DANNY QUANTUM AND THE NUCLEAR DETONATOR

RON SARIG

TABLE OF CONTENTS

CHAPTER 1. The Safe 1

CHAPTER 2. The Scientist 5

CHAPTER 3. Daniel 9

CHAPTER 4. The Committee of Three 17

CHAPTER 5. The Special Talent and Schrödinger's Cat 23

CHAPTER 6. Geography 27

CHAPTER 7. Special Theory of Relativity 31

CHAPTER 8. Schrödinger 35

CHAPTER 9. First Mission 41

CHAPTER 10. Danny becomes "Schrödinger" 51

CHAPTER 11. The Archive 59

CHAPTER 12. Operation Operetta 65

CHAPTER 13. Kryptonite 71

CHAPTER 14. Operation Elul 83

CHAPTER 15. The Nuclear Detonator 89

CHAPTER 16. Operation Elul Returns 99

CHAPTER 17. Epilogue and Perhaps a Beginning 115

CHAPTER ONE:
THE SAFE

That morning, like every other morning, the entrance was tightly guarded. In the lobby, five massive guards stood watch, each armed with Russian-made submachine guns specially adapted for close quarters. These weapons could unleash twelve bullets per second—enough firepower to neutralize any intruder daring to force their way inside.

The guards, clad in olive uniforms, were towering figures, each appearing to weigh over 100 kilos. Ceramic vests covered their chests, capable of stopping 9mm bullets. Lightweight but durable metal helmets protected their heads, complete with visors that allowed them to see perfectly in total darkness. Tiny radio devices kept them connected to the control room and each other. On their right legs were holsters carrying forged-steel commando knives, and their necks bore identical tattoos—a mark of their elite status in the "Zurkhaneh," a martial arts school rooted in the "Pahlevani" doctrine. Each guard held the highest rank in this ancient discipline.

The lobby they guarded lay at the end of a long, narrow

corridor, secured by two thick steel doors reminiscent of a bank vault. Only one door could open at a time; when one opened, the other locked automatically. The guards could seal the doors with a single button press. Cameras, motion detectors, and sound sensors monitored the corridor. Any unauthorized person attempting entry would be trapped between the steel doors, where the system could deploy sedative gas, emit paralyzing sound waves, or even electrify the floor tiles to incapacitate the intruder without a fight.

Few citizens of the Republic even knew this building existed, and fewer still understood its purpose. Fewer than ten people were privy to its secrets, all of them close associates of the Supreme Leader. Only this select group could pass the guards, navigate the trap-filled corridor, and reach the building's inner sanctum safely.

At the end of the corridor was the security room—a fortress in itself. Its walls, floor, and ceiling were constructed from reinforced concrete 1.5 meters thick and coated in a steel alloy. The door was explosion-proof, secured with combination locks and a steel bolt system. Inside, a German-engineered safe protected the Republic's most closely guarded secrets. This state-of-the-art safe featured a randomly changing electronic code, biometric retina identification, and a door reinforced to withstand at least an hour of drilling or cutting—enough time for commando units stationed nearby to intervene.

Inside the safe were documents detailing the Supreme Leader's hidden wealth, valued at over $100 billion. This fortune, concealed under the façade of an innocent-sounding company called "Setad," was entirely under his control. These resources allowed the Supreme Leader to consolidate power, buy loyalty, crush opposition, and expand his influence.

No one had ever breached the building. Attempts by elite organizations like the CIA, GRU, and MI6 had all failed. Those who tried were either captured or killed, never to return home.

That morning, precisely at 10:00 a.m., the alarm blared. The cameras revealed nothing unusual. Neither motion nor sound detectors picked up any disturbances. Even the vibration and temperature sensors embedded in the security room's walls remained silent. Yet, the doors to the corridor and security room automatically locked, sealing the building. The security unit commander stood in the control room, his eyes glued to the monitors. Everything seemed normal—except for one chilling detail.

On the vault room's security feed, he saw something that made his heart stop. A cold sweat broke out across his skin as his breath caught in his throat. His mind screamed in terror.

The guards were unconscious, sprawled across the floor.

The safe door was wide open.

And the metal box that had been inside—the box holding the Supreme Leader's most closely guarded secrets—was empty.

Ron Sarig

CHAPTER TWO:
THE SCIENTIST

In the Abu-Tor neighborhood of Jerusalem, the Professor sat in his cozy armchair, nestled in the middle of his home library. Across from him, his guest sat quietly, waiting. Bookshelves packed to the brim surrounded them on every wall, Filling the room with a sense of knowledge. In the center of the room stood a large wooden table, completely covered in stacks of books, their spines revealing titles on physics, biology, chemistry, mathematics, astronomy, and countless other subjects.

The Professor, though well into his eighties, was anything but frail. His sharp eyes and quick mind were legendary, particularly in his field of expertise—quantum mechanics. Despite his age, he was always up-to-date, staying ahead of even the youngest minds in the exact sciences.

"What were we talking about?" the Professor asked suddenly, breaking the silence. His guest gave a small, knowing smile but said nothing.

"Ah, yes, I remember now," the Professor continued.

"We were discussing the last operation... and yes, I know, everything is highly classified and hush-hush, but I understand it went well."

"It went fine," the guest replied with a hint of a smile. "I mean, I'm here, aren't I?"

"And how did it go with your... unique talent?" the Professor asked, leaning forward slightly.

"That's why I came," the guest said, his tone growing serious. "There's something I need to tell you—something I need your thoughts on."

The Professor straightened in his chair. "Go on."

"I'm not sure how to explain it," the guest began, pausing to choose his words carefully. "When I used my talent, I felt... something. A disturbance. It didn't cause any problems, but it was strange. I've never felt anything like it before, and I think we need to figure out what it was."

"Do you think it was deliberate?" the Professor asked, his sharp gaze locking onto the guest.

"I don't know. Maybe."

"Tell me exactly what happened," the Professor pressed.

The guest nodded. "You know how sometimes, when you're tired or unwell, your vision gets blurry or doubles? Like, for a second, everything splits, then snaps back into focus? Do you know what I mean?"

"Of course," the Professor said with a slight wave of his hand. "It's a common enough phenomenon. Did you see double?"

"No," the guest said, frowning. "I didn't see double—I felt

double. It was like my body... split, just for a fraction of a second, and then came back together. It wasn't visual; it was physical. I've never experienced anything like it before when using my talent."

The Professor leaned back, his brow furrowed in thought. Moments passed in silence, the only sound the faint creak of the armchair as the Professor shifted. The guest waited patiently, watching the old man process this new information.

Finally, the Professor stirred, as if waking from a dream. "This might be significant," he said slowly. "I'll need to run some calculations and tests in the lab. It will take time. Meanwhile, you must be cautious."

The guest chuckled softly. "I'm always cautious."

They stood and shook hands. "I know the way," the guest said. "I'll see myself out. Goodbye."

The Professor watched him go, his mind already spinning with theories and possibilities.

Ron Sarig

CHAPTER THREE:
DANIEL

Daniel, who was always just called Danny, always knew there was something strange about him. From a young age, strange things happened to him.

He had odd dreams. Dreams that none of his friends had. He dreamed he was in two places at the same time.

When his mother said she was worried about his father not coming home at the usual time, he would close his eyes and dream that he was with his father near the bus station, then open his eyes and tell his mother: "Don't worry mom, dad is waiting for the bus and he'll be here soon." His mother would laugh and say "Danny, Danny, you and your dreams again." And when dad arrived home saying "The bus was fifteen minutes late," mom would look at Danny and say "Why don't you dream about the lottery numbers? We could be rich by now."

When he was in fourth grade, the teacher said she'd give an 'Excellent' to any student who knew the answer to the question - "Which month was the Jewish New Year during biblical times?" All the kids thought about the answer, and Danny closed his eyes and dreamed.

He dreamed he was in the library and the librarian revealed the answer to him. When he opened his eyes, he knew the answer, but the teacher said he'd only get a 'Very Good' because she didn't like students falling asleep during class, even if just for a moment.

And there were other strange things. He knew what people were talking about even when they were very far from him. He could bring various objects very quickly even though he didn't excel in running competitions.

But the strangest thing was that they could never photograph him properly. In all pictures, his figure appeared blurry.

Although Danny's mom and dad were religious and observant people, they didn't believe in miracles. At age thirteen, just before his Bar Mitzvah, Danny's parents decided it was time to check exactly what was happening with their son.

The family doctor examined Danny from head to toe and said: "Everything's fine, Danny is perfectly healthy, you have nothing to worry about."

But Danny's parents were still not at ease, so they took him to another doctor and even to a psychologist who said: "Danny is an intelligent and normal child, everything is fine with him and there's nothing to worry about."

Danny's parents relaxed.

A few days after visiting the psychologist, there was a "capture the flag" competition at the "Bnei Akiva" branch, the youth movement that Danny and his friends were part of. Each group had to try to take the opposing group's flag and bring it to their territory.

Less than two minutes into the game, Danny appeared with the rival group's flag in his hand. This was strange and even a bit frightening because no one saw him running or sneaking or doing anything at all. But Danny was the hero of the day.

The next day, everyone in the "moshav" was talking about Danny and the successful trick, which no one understood exactly how it was done.

That day, Danny's mother said to his father: "This is no joke, we must do something about the child." Danny's father, not knowing what to do, called his older brother who held an important position in the municipality, and asked if he knew someone who could help.

Danny's uncle called his friend from army days, who was the deputy director of "Barzilai" Hospital in Ashdod, who scheduled an appointment for Danny and his parents with the head of the hospital's neurological department, who is an expert in brain and nervous system.

Dr. Lipschitz received Danny and his parents in his office.

Danny looked around. On the right wall hung framed certificates with large stamps in foreign languages. On the left wall hung photographs, and next to them was a large drawing of something that looked like a bunch of grapes after someone had eaten all the grapes.

Dr. Lipschitz looked at Danny and picked up a metal pen from his desk, pulling out an extending pointer.

"These are brain scans," he told Danny. "This is the right lobe and this is the left." He pointed with the pointer pen.

Danny remained silent.

"And what's this? A bunch of grapes?" asked Danny, pointing to the drawing.

"That's a drawing of the nervous system," said Dr. Lipschitz and laughed.

Dr. Lipschitz scheduled tests for Danny. Some tests were done in the doctor's or nurse's room, but some were conducted in other rooms in the hospital with large machines with strange names like "CT" and "MRI" and even a machine called "fMRI" which is a machine that can detect whether the brain is functioning properly and whether any brain functions have been impaired.

Before entering the first test, Dr. Lipschitz introduced Danny to the technician who would help conduct the tests.

The technician brought Danny into the room and showed him the machine and explained its different parts and how they work.

And so, Danny learned that these machines send sound waves and electromagnetic waves into the human body without harming it.

These waves return from the human body as echoes and are captured and recorded by special software in the computer, which collects and processes the information and converts it into an image.

The images would be sent to another specialist doctor called a "radiologist." The radiologist knows how to interpret the computer-generated images and explain them in a way that allows the doctor to understand exactly what's happening in the examined body part.

Danny lay quietly through all the tests, as the machines creaked and hummed and moved forward and backward, up and down, and flashed with all kinds of lights.

Toward evening, when the last test was completed, Danny and his parents drove back home to the "moshav".

After several days, Doctor Lipschitz called Danny's father.

"Danny is healthy and there's no reason to worry, but there is still something important you need to know," he said and asked them to come meet with him at the hospital.

On the appointed day, they all sat in Doctor Lipschitz's office. Along with the doctor came an elderly man whom they hadn't met before.

Doctor Lipschitz looked at Danny's parents and said, "As I already mentioned in our phone conversation, Danny is healthy and you have no reason to worry."

"Then how do you explain all the strange things he does?" asked Danny's mother.

"Well," said the doctor, "I still can't explain everything but we did find something different about Danny." He looked at the parents and asked, "Have you ever heard of the term 'DNA'?"

"No," said Danny's mother and father together.

"Well," said Doctor Lipschitz with a smile, "I won't give you a course in molecular biology now, but DNA is the code that determines how the building blocks that make up the human body are arranged.

You could say it's like a building plan or like a cake recipe.

Although every person has their own special and unique

DNA, there is a certain order for everyone. And this is exactly what I want to explain to you.

In the tests we did on Danny, we discovered that Danny's DNA is arranged slightly differently from that of other people, and this might be what causes the strange phenomena you told me about.

This doesn't mean he's sick, God forbid, or that something's wrong with him, but rather shows that he is special and unique.

Danny's uniqueness piqued our curiosity, and so that we can all understand the matter, I asked my good friend to join our meeting and explain.

Dr. Lipschitz pointed to the elderly man sitting next to him and said, "Meet Professor Wittgenstein."

Professor Wittgenstein is the number one expert in the country and perhaps in the world in quantum theory, and if anyone can understand what's happening with Danny, he's the man."

Danny's parents shifted their gaze from Dr. Lipschitz to the man sitting next to him.

"Nice to meet you," said Professor Wittgenstein and smiled.

"I'm sure you're confused and maybe even worried, but I believe I have answers to your questions.

Unfortunately, the answers might be a bit complicated to understand, but I'll try to explain in a way we can all understand. And first, I want to reassure you, what Danny has is a gift, not an illness."

Danny's mother breathed a sigh of relief.

Prof. Wittgenstein looked at her and continued. "I'd like to ask you, Danny's mother, did anything unusual happen while you were pregnant with Danny?"

Danny's mother thought for a moment and said "No, everything was normal,

I wasn't sick and all the tests I had at the well-baby clinic and with my doctor were fine."

"In that case, the most likely possibility is that during cell division in the early embryonic stage, a random mutation occurred in the DNA editing. Such mutations aren't rare in themselves, but they usually only survive for a short time and disappear on their own. This mutation apparently managed to survive the evolutionary process and created the change in Danny's DNA structure."

"But how does that explain anything?" asked Danny's father.

"Well," Professor Wittgenstein cleared his throat, "I'm not entirely sure but it's possible that Danny is able to enter and exit a state of 'superposition.'"

"Super what?" asked Danny's mother, in a hoarse throat.

"Let me try to explain," said Prof. Wittgenstein. "Think about baking a cake. You've finished preparing the dough and now you need to decide if you want a chocolate cake or a cheesecake.

At that moment, before you decide which cake you want to make, the cake you'll prepare could be either a chocolate cake or a cheesecake, it can be two different things. Only after you decide what you want and add either chocolate or cheese to the mixture will the cake become either a chocolate cake or a cheesecake."

"What nonsense is this?" Danny's father grew angry, "He's a child, not a cake."

"True," said the Professor, "but Danny is special. Danny can be two things at the same time, just like the cake can be cheese or chocolate before you decide what to do with it.

But let me share something more important with you. Science has never encountered such a phenomenon before.

As far as we know, there is no one else in the world with such an ability, and if you'll take our advice, for Danny to grow up like any normal child, you and we must ensure that no one knows about his special talent.

No one must be told about this. Danny will also need to keep it a secret.

The gift he received, if used incorrectly, could turn into a curse."

CHAPTER FOUR:
THE COMMITTEE OF THREE

Inside the room sat four people: the Prime Minister, the Head of the Mossad (Israel's Institute for Intelligence and Special Operations), the Chairman of the Atomic Energy Committee, and a fourth individual wearing a mask.

The committee members knew the masked man only by his code name. Among the three committee members, only the Head of the Mossad knew his real identity and what he looked like.

The room appeared to be an ordinary conference room, but it was equipped with a Faraday device—a specialized installation designed to block all electrical fields and prevent any form of external eavesdropping.

The Prime Minister, the Head of the Mossad, and the Chairman of the Atomic Energy Committee comprised a secretive group known as "The Committee of Three," created for one purpose only: deploying the covert operative code-named "Schrödinger."

Schrödinger was activated exclusively for critical operations aimed at neutralizing significant threats to Israel's security. The committee met monthly in a discreet government facility located near the Mediterranean coast, not far from Ashkelon. During each meeting, the Head of the Mossad presented a list of potential missions, and the committee decided whether any warranted Schrödinger's deployment.

The existence of Agent Schrödinger and his unique abilities was a closely guarded state secret. The committee approved his missions only in the most extreme circumstances, as exposing Schrödinger would mean losing one of Israel's most valuable security assets.

"We're here today to receive a report on the latest operation: breaking into the Supreme Leader's safe," began the Prime Minister, who also served as the committee's chairman.

"We acquired the intelligence we needed," said the Head of the Mossad. "We already knew they were close to producing a nuclear bomb, but the information Schrödinger retrieved from the safe confirmed they're even closer to completing the nuclear detonator. Without the detonator, all the enriched uranium in the Bushehr reactor is useless. Last month, their experts traveled to North Korea and received detailed blueprints for building the detonator necessary to trigger an atomic chain reaction."

"Why would North Korea give them such information? What's in it for them?" the Prime Minister asked.

"Oil. A lot of it," replied the Head of the Mossad. "North

Korea is poor, facing a harsh winter, and desperately needs resources to survive."

The Chairman of the Atomic Energy Committee turned to Schrödinger. "I understand how you accessed the vault room, but how did you bypass the random password mechanism and obtain a matching retina scan?"

"The password was the easy part," Schrödinger replied. "As you know, every nation is racing to develop a quantum computer capable of breaking any encryption in seconds."

"That's true," said the Chairman, "but no country has a functioning quantum computer yet."

"Also true," Schrödinger said with a faint smile. "But if you have millions of people entering random passwords simultaneously, you can brute force your way past any mechanism within minutes."

"But you don't have millions of people..." the Chairman began, then stopped abruptly... "Oh. I see. Now I understand."

"And the retina scan?" the Chairman pressed. "How did you manage that?"

"Luck," Schrödinger admitted. "Do you remember the Republic's President's helicopter crash back in May?"

"Yes, of course. The President was on board during the crash."

"And do you recall how rescue teams didn't reach the site until sixteen hours later?"

"Yes. The crash happened in a remote, mountainous area. It was difficult to locate and access the site. The entire world was waiting to see if the President survived."

"Well," Schrödinger continued, "not everyone struggled to get there. Those who arrived first had access to two intact retinas. The crash damage to the body was extensive, so no one questioned why the retinas were missing."

"And because the new President wasn't elected for nearly three months," Schrödinger explained, "the old retina scans were still active in the security system. Nobody thought to replace them, as no one expected retinas from a deceased individual to be used."

The Prime Minister nodded. "Thank you, Schrödinger. On behalf of the State of Israel, I want to commend you for another successful mission."

"Always at your service," Schrödinger replied, shaking the Prime Minister's hand before leaving the room.

Once outside, Schrödinger removed his mask, got into his car, and drove carefully northward toward Tel Aviv.

Back inside the room, the Prime Minister turned to the others. "Now we must address the nuclear detonator problem. If they complete it, they'll have a functional bomb. We can't let that happen. We must act."

The Head of the Mossad spoke up. "Immediately after receiving Schrödinger's intel, I flew to Washington and met with the National Security Advisor. He was as shocked as we were and promised to raise the issue with the President."

"But the President is in the middle of an election campaign," the Prime Minister said. "He's a 'lame duck' with limited political power to authorize an attack."

"Exactly," the Mossad chief agreed. "Until the election is over, the U.S. won't be able to form an international coalition to deal with this threat. And we can't afford to wait. By then, it may be too late."

"So what are our options?" the Prime Minister asked.

"The detonator is being developed in an underground facility near Shahdad," the Mossad chief explained. "We could try to bomb the site using our new F-35s, but the facility is deep in enemy territory. Reaching it would require crossing their airspace, which could escalate into war."

"Can't we sabotage the facility with another computer worm, like the one we used on their enrichment turbines?" asked the Chairman.

"We don't have the time," the Mossad chief replied. "The equipment is already on-site. Even if we succeeded, it would only cause a delay."

"Then we'll have to take the risk and bomb the facility," the Prime Minister decided. "I'll speak with the Defense Minister and Chief of Staff to prepare an immediate plan."

The meeting adjourned, and the three men left the room to begin their work.

Ron Sarig

CHAPTER FIVE:
THE SPECIAL TALENT AND SCHRÖDINGER'S CAT

A few days before his Bar Mitzvah, Danny sat in Professor Wittgenstein's vast library.

"Did your mom and dad explain to you why you can do all these strange things?" asked the Professor.

"They tried," Danny replied, "but I didn't understand anything. In the end, they just told me not to talk about it with anyone, and that kind of scared me."

"I'm not surprised," the Professor said. "What you have is so unique that no one in the world has ever seen or heard of anything like it. Your talent is extraordinary, and the possibilities it presents are almost limitless. But what's important for you to understand right now is that while your ability is rare, it's not magic or a miracle. It's a scientifically explainable phenomenon, even if it's extremely unusual."

"Can you explain it to me?" Danny asked eagerly.

"I'll try," the Professor said. "But keep in mind, some of this might be a bit complicated."

The Professor leaned back in his chair. "You probably know that when a fetus begins forming in its mother's womb, it starts as a single cell. That cell divides into two, then four, and so on until billions of cells form a complete human body. This process is controlled by a sort of program inside the cell called DNA. It determines whether a cell becomes a muscle, bone, or part of an organ.

"With billions of cell divisions, mistakes sometimes happen—like a glitch in a computer program. These mistakes, or mutations, can create unexpected changes. We believe your unique ability comes from one of these mutations."

"So I'm a mutant?" Danny asked, his eyes wide. "Like in the X-Men movies?"

The Professor chuckled. "Not quite. You're perfectly healthy, Danny. Your cells are just a little different, and that difference allows you to do something extraordinary—exist in more than one place at the same time. That's how you could be in your team's tent during the flag game while also sneaking into the rival team's camp to grab their flag."

Danny blinked. "But how does that even work? Do I split into two? And what if I don't come back together? Would there be two of me?"

"Those are excellent questions," said the Professor with a smile. "Let me try to explain, though it might get a bit tricky.

"You don't actually split into two. You, Danny, remain one person. What happens is that you exist simultaneously in two places—a phenomenon explained by quantum theory."

Danny frowned. "Quantum theory?"

The Professor nodded. "It's a complex field of science. Let me tell you about a thought experiment by a famous scientist named Schrödinger. He used it to illustrate how something can exist in two states at once. It involves a cat."

"A cat?" Danny asked, raising an eyebrow. "Like a real cat? One that chases mice?"

"Exactly," the Professor said with a smile. "Schrödinger imagined a sealed box containing a cat and a single radioactive atom. If the atom decayed during the experiment, it would release radiation that would kill the cat. If the atom didn't decay, the cat would stay alive. The twist is that, until the box is opened, the cat is considered both alive and dead at the same time. This idea is called quantum superposition."

Danny leaned forward, fascinated. "So, when I exist in two places, am I like Schrödinger's cat? Half alive and half dead?"

"Not at all," the Professor assured him. "You're entirely alive. But like the cat, you're in two states—or two places—simultaneously."

"But how do I know what the other me is doing?" Danny asked after a moment of thought.

"Good question," said the Professor. "This is where quantum entanglement comes in. It's a connection between particles that allows them to share information instantly, no matter how far apart they are. In your case, it's as though the two versions of you are entangled, working together as one."

Danny grinned. "Entanglement? Like when girls braid their hair?"

The Professor laughed. "Exactly! But in quantum physics, it's much more complicated."

Danny sat back, processing everything. "It sounds cool, but why can't I tell my friends about it?"

"Because with great power comes great responsibility," the Professor said seriously. "Your talent is a gift, but it must be used wisely. If the wrong people found out about it, they might try to use you for evil purposes."

Danny swallowed hard. "Evil? Like what?"

The Professor sighed. "Imagine if criminals knew you could enter a bank vault and take all the money without being caught. People would try to exploit your abilities for their own gain."

Danny nodded slowly. "I understand. I'll stop using it just for fun."

The Professor smiled. "Good. In time, we'll develop your ability further. You could do great things, Danny—not just for yourself, but for Israel, and maybe even the whole world."

"I'll do my best," Danny said, his expression determined.

"Good. Now, how about some pizza?" the Professor asked with a wink.

When the pizza arrived, Danny couldn't resist using his talent one last time to swap the olives for mushrooms. As the Professor frowned in confusion, Danny grinned mischievously. They both laughed and enjoyed their meal.

"Don't forget to practice your 'Haftarah'," the Professor reminded him. "We'll talk more after your Bar Mitzvah."

Danny smiled. "Thanks, Professor. See you next week!"

CHAPTER SIX:
GEOGRAPHY

Professor Wittgenstein was a member of Israel's Atomic Energy Committee, tasked with advising the government on advancing nuclear research and development. One day, he met privately with Mr. Gershon Plank, the Committee Chairman, to present his theory about Danny's extraordinary talent and its potential for science and the state.

Professor Wittgenstein proposed studying and researching the phenomenon, suggesting that it could someday lead to groundbreaking advancements. The Committee Chairman agreed, authorizing the use of the Nuclear Research Center's resources for the research. They also decided to keep the discovery secret for now, presenting it publicly as a youth science enrichment program.

After Danny's Bar Mitzvah, Professor Wittgenstein approached Danny's parents with an idea. He suggested enrolling Danny in a special after-school program at the Nuclear Research Center in Nahal Sorek, just a fifteen-minute drive from their home. He described it as a program for gifted students, offering exciting experiences and hands-on experiments in the center's laboratories.

While this was true, it wasn't the whole truth. The real purpose of the program was to help Danny develop greater control over his unique abilities and push them to their maximum potential, all while assisting the Professor's research.

Danny began meeting with Professor Wittgenstein twice a week in the afternoons.

"Today, we'll learn geography," said the Professor.

"Geography?" Danny asked, puzzled. "What does that have to do with anything?"

"Well," the Professor began, "in everyday life, when you want to get somewhere, you need to know two things: where you are and where you want to go. For example, if you're at home and want to go to school, you already know the route because you've walked it before. You know where there's a hill, where there's a shortcut, and so on. Geography is the foundation for planning your journey."

Danny nodded slowly.

"Now, the same principle applies when you want to be in more than one place at the same time," the Professor continued. "So far, you've only gone to places you could see or places you already knew. For instance, when you grabbed the flag during the game, you could see the opposing team's tent and go straight there. Or when you visited the library to ask about Jewish New Year traditions, you already knew where the library was.

"But what happens if you need to get to a place you've never been? Let's say I ask you to be here and at the Jerusalem Zoo at the same time. You might end up somewhere random in Jerusalem, like the Western Wall, because that's a place you know. But getting to the zoo? That's a different challenge."

"So how do I get to a place I don't know?" Danny asked.

"With coordinates," the Professor replied.

"Coordinates?" Danny repeated, intrigued.

"Exactly. You've seen maps in geography class, right? The ones with lines running up and down and side to side?"

Danny nodded again.

"The vertical lines are called longitude, and the horizontal ones are latitude. The point where they intersect is called a coordinate or reference point—RP for short. Every location on Earth has its own RP."

"And if I know the RP of a place, I can get there?" Danny asked.

"Not quite," the Professor said, rolling out a large world map. "Take a look at this map. See how each rectangle between the lines represents a large area? Near the equator, a single rectangle can measure over 100 kilometers across. That's like the distance from here to 'Zichron Yaakov'. It's not precise enough if you want to reach a specific spot within that rectangle."

"So, what do we do?" Danny asked.

"We use more precise coordinates. Longitude and latitude are divided into degrees—360 lines each. But to get finer details, we divide each degree into 60 smaller parts called minutes. And each minute is further divided into 60 seconds. That gives us much smaller units, but even seconds leave room for error—about 31 meters. That's not good enough for certain tasks."

"So what's the solution?"

"We use decimal coordinates," the Professor explained. "With six decimal places, we can narrow it down to an error margin of about 10 centimeters. That level of precision is usually enough."

Danny listened carefully, though some of the explanation still felt overwhelming.

"And what do I do with these coordinates?" he asked.

"Our brains are naturally good at calculating routes," the Professor said. "If you know where you are and where you want to go, your mind can figure out the path."

"But what if I want to reach an airplane in the sky?" Danny asked.

"Excellent question!" the Professor exclaimed, clearly delighted. "That's where three-dimensional coordinates come in. In addition to longitude and latitude, we also consider altitude. It's like throwing a basketball. When you pass the ball to a teammate, the ball travels along the court in two dimensions—length and width. But if you want to shoot a basket, you need to aim for a specific height as well. The same concept applies to reaching an airplane."

"So I need to imagine an arrow pointing from me to my destination?" Danny asked.

"Exactly," the Professor said, smiling. "Your brain and your special abilities will handle the rest. And now, your shuttle is waiting to take you home. See you next week."

"Goodbye," Danny said with a wave.

CHAPTER SEVEN:

SPECIAL THEORY OF RELATIVITY

The Professor and Danny sat once again in the laboratory at the Nuclear Research Center in Nahal Sorek. "How was your week?" the Professor asked Danny.

"Normal. Nothing special," Danny replied. "I've been thinking about what we discussed last week, and I really want to try reaching all kinds of new places."

"I understand," said the Professor, "but you need to realize that the brain is like a muscle. To get it to work exactly how we want, we have to train it, just like weightlifting. You start with a small weight, maybe one kilogram, and slowly increase the load so your muscles can grow stronger and more resilient with training. We'll start with short distances and gradually increase them. Also, remember—you don't want to end up stranded on a deserted island in the middle of the ocean without a boat to bring you back."

"There's something else I don't understand," Danny said.

"Just one thing?" the Professor teased, smiling.

"Well, no, but never mind. I have a question."

"What's your question?"

"You explained that even though I can be in two places at once, I'm still the same Danny."

"Correct," the Professor confirmed.

"So how is it that I talked to the librarian for five minutes, but in class, nothing seemed to happen? When I opened my eyes, it felt like everything continued from the exact second I closed them."

"Once again, a smart and insightful question," the Professor said with a smile. "And as always, the explanation is simple. Have you ever heard of the Theory of Relativity?"

"No," Danny replied.

"Hmmm," the Professor mused. "Let's see if I can explain it in a way that makes sense. Do you remember when I told you about the genius scientist Albert Einstein? Over ninety years ago, in 1905, Einstein published a groundbreaking scientific idea called the 'Special Theory of Relativity.'"

"What's a theory?" Danny asked. "My older cousin says he's studying 'theory' to get his driver's license, but I don't think he's a genius."

"You're right, Danny. The word 'theory' can mean different things. In your cousin's case, 'theory' refers to the written test required for a driver's license, as opposed to the practical driving test. But Einstein's theory is a scientific hypothesis, a way to explain phenomena in the world. For example, when people noticed that clothes dry faster in summer than in winter, they formed a theory: higher temperatures cause water to evaporate more quickly. Experiments confirmed this. If you heat water to 100 degrees, it boils, turns to steam, and eventually evaporates completely. Without heat, water will still evaporate, but much more slowly, depending on the surrounding air temperature."

"Einstein's theory," the Professor continued, "explains a strange phenomenon. Imagine you're moving in a car, and at the exact same moment, two lights are turned on—one in front of you, in the direction you're heading, and one behind you, in the direction you came from. Both lights are the same distance away. Yet, you'll see the light in front of you first."

"Why is that strange?" Danny asked. "If we're moving toward the front light and away from the back light, of course we'd see the front light first."

"Ah," said the Professor, "but what I didn't tell you is that these lights are moving too—at the same speed and in the same direction as you. The distance between you and each light stays exactly the same."

"That doesn't make sense," Danny said. "Are you saying the light from the front is faster than the light from the back? Maybe the front light is bigger or stronger?"

"A good guess," the Professor replied, "but here's the twist: even before Einstein's time, scientists discovered that the speed of light is constant. It doesn't change, no matter the source or observer."

"Then someone's cheating," Danny declared.

"No cheating," the Professor assured him. "Einstein's theory explains that time itself is relative to the observer. If

I'm standing still while you're moving, the faster you go, the slower your time will pass compared to mine. If you were moving at the speed of light, from my perspective, your time wouldn't progress at all."

"So," the Professor concluded, "because you can be in two places at once, time progresses very, very slowly for someone watching you in class, allowing you to spend what feels like five minutes talking to the librarian. But remember, if you stay in this special state for too long, time will eventually progress in both places, even if it's just a little."

CHAPTER EIGHT:
SCHRÖDINGER

Danny and his parents stood in Churchill Auditorium at the Technion in Haifa. An excited Danny held his bachelor's degree certificate in Materials Engineering.

"You're already twenty-six," his mother said, "and your father and I really want to know what your plans are now that you've finished your studies."

"I'm planning to take a long trip to South America with the guys from my platoon, and then we'll see," Danny replied.

"What's in South America for you?" his mother asked. "Why don't you find a job in your field, meet a nice girl, and settle down? Your father and I are already dreaming of grandchildren running around our yard at the moshav."

"Don't worry, Mom," Danny laughed. "'To everything, there is a season, and a time for every purpose,' as Ecclesiastes says. But after four years in infantry and another four years at the Technion—honestly, I'm not sure which was harder—I need to clear my head."

"Well," his mother sighed in disappointment, "you should know that Yardena's daughter, who lives at the end of the street, is very nice, and she's already a doctor—"

"Enough, Mom," Danny interrupted. "Stop trying to match me up. I can manage just fine on my own."

"Fine," she said, relenting. "I made you a box of your favorite Yemenite soup, just the way you like it."

"You spoil me too much," Danny said, grinning. "What girl would want me with a belly like a pregnant woman's?"

"When are you leaving?" his mother asked.

"In a week. I have a few things to take care of first, and tomorrow, I need to meet the Professor in Tel Aviv."

The next day, Danny drove to Tel Aviv. His meeting took place in an apartment on the third floor of a building on Maze Street, across from the Diaghilev Hotel.

He knocked on the door of apartment number five, and the Professor opened it. "I'm happy to see you," the Professor said. "Come in and meet Moshe."

Danny shook hands with Moshe, whose real name wasn't actually Moshe, "Nice to meet you. I'm Danny."

"I know," Moshe said. "I've been following your progress for a long time, and I'm glad we're finally meeting."

Danny frowned, surprised, but said nothing.

"Sit, sit," the Professor said. "What would you like to drink?"

"Just a glass of water," Danny replied.

The Professor placed a glass of water on the small coffee

table near Danny and cleared his throat. "First, congratulations on completing your studies," he said.

"Thank you," Danny said.

"I invited you here today because Moshe has an offer for you," the Professor continued.

"An offer? My mom has plenty of offers for me too. I hope this isn't one of those," Danny joked.

The Professor chuckled. "No, this is a very different kind of offer. Moshe is from the Mossad, and he has something important to discuss with you."

"The Mossad?" Danny asked with a smirk. "Isn't that for spies?"

"The Institute for Intelligence and Special Operations does more than spy work," Moshe replied, smiling. "We want you to join us."

"And what would you want me to do?" Danny asked. "I have a degree in Materials Engineering and Physics. That doesn't sound like something you'd need."

"Oh, we do," Moshe said. "After all, we're the ones who secretly funded your scholarship. We believe you can use your skills in both your field and to help protect Israel's security. Your education, combined with the special abilities you developed under Professor Wittgenstein, make you uniquely qualified."

"You'll join a unit called Libertad," Moshe continued, "which focuses on technological innovation. Occasionally, if a critical security need arises, we'll ask you to use your special abilities to neutralize threats and secure crucial information or materials."

"My special talent?" Danny said, wrinkling his nose. "I haven't thought about it in years, except for that one time in November 2012 during Operation Pillar of Defense. A rocket from Gaza hit the building I was in with my platoon, and I used my ability to neutralize its detonator. Otherwise, it would've killed us all."

"I remember," Moshe said. "The newspapers called it a miracle."

"It's like riding a bike," the Professor said. "Once you start practicing again, it'll come back naturally. We didn't train you during your adolescence because we wanted you to have a normal life—serve in the army, go to university, and live like anyone else. But now it's time to make a decision."

"Go on your trip to South America," Moshe said. "When you come back in three months, we'll start. No one will know about your abilities except for me and the Professor. Officially, you'll be working on technological developments in your field. You can live a normal, quiet life until we need you. Your code name will be Schrödinger."

"See you in three months," Moshe said, standing to leave.

After he left, Danny looked at the Professor. "You planned this thirteen years ago when we first met, didn't you?"

"Not exactly," the Professor replied. "The idea came later, after I saw your intelligence and bravery. Your talent is extraordinary—a gift that shouldn't be wasted."

Danny sighed. "I feel like I've been set up. I never asked for this, and now I'm stuck with it. I hope it won't be a Pandora's box."

"Guns don't kill people," the Professor said. "Only those

who pull the trigger do. Your power is like a gun, and I know you'll only use it for good."

"Let's hope so," Danny said. "See you in three months. I'm looking forward to applying what I learned at the Technion in the lab."

"Goodbye, Danny," the Professor said.

"Goodbye," Danny replied as he left.

Ron Sarig

CHAPTER NINE:
FIRST MISSION

"It's been a month since you returned from abroad and started working with us in the 'Libertad' unit," the Head of the Mossad said to Danny. "How are you adjusting?"

"Pretty well," Danny replied. "The lab work is fascinating, and the team has been very welcoming."

"I'm glad to hear that," Shamir said. "But now it's time to test your special talent. I understand you haven't used it in quite some time and might be a bit rusty."

"True," Danny admitted, "but Professor Wittgenstein said it's like riding a bicycle, so I hope that's true."

"We've prepared a training program for you," Shamir explained. "The goal is first to ensure you still have control over your ability. Once you're comfortable 'riding this bicycle,' we'll work together to explore your limits—what you can and cannot do. The program was designed with Professor Wittgenstein's input and is similar to training for an athlete preparing for the World Championships. We'll start small and gradually increase the difficulty. Each morning, you'll complete one or more tasks, then return to your regular lab work."

Shamir handed Danny a sheet of paper. "This is tomorrow's program. Read it, then destroy it—we don't want anyone else seeing it. I'll give you the next day's mission each morning."

Danny glanced at the paper and smiled. "Understood. I'll take care of it," he said.

The next morning, at 8:05 a.m., Danny arrived at Shamir's office.

"Hello, Dina," he said to the office manager. "I have some papers to deliver to the boss."

Dina picked up the phone and said, "There's someone here named Danny with papers for you."

After a moment, she put the receiver down. "Go ahead; he's waiting for you," she said.

Danny entered and handed Shamir three ATM withdrawal receipts, each showing a withdrawal of 100 shekels. The withdrawals were dated that morning, with times of 8:00 a.m., 8:02 a.m., and 8:04 a.m.

Shamir opened his browser and entered the branch numbers printed on the receipts: 478 Ben Yehuda Street, 421 Gan Ha'ir on Ibn Gabirol Street, and 405 Kikar Hamedina on Weizmann Street.

"And here are the 300 shekels," Danny said, handing him three bills. "You can check the serial numbers if you want—they match the receipts and were withdrawn from three different branches."

"Good," Shamir said. "Tomorrow's mission will be similar.

Bring me 300 shekels from ATMs in three different cities: 'Kiryat Shmona', 'Netanya', and 'Be'er Sheva'."

The next morning, at 8:13 a.m., Danny returned to Shamir's office. Dina didn't bother asking questions this time. "Go in; he's waiting for you," she said with a smile.

Danny handed Shamir three receipts and 300 shekels. The receipts showed withdrawals that morning at 8:00 a.m., 8:02 a.m., and 8:09 a.m., from branches in Kiryat Shmona, Netanya, and Be'er Sheva.

Shamir reviewed the receipts and noted the times. "Good," he said, "but why did it take you seven minutes between Netanya and Be'er Sheva?"

"There was a line," Danny explained with a grin. "An elderly woman needed help remembering her code."

Shamir chuckled. "Tomorrow, we'll raise the stakes. You'll perform the mission while remaining here in my office."

The next morning, at 8:00 a.m. sharp, Danny arrived. Dina greeted him warmly. "Good morning, Danny. He's waiting for you."

Danny entered, and Shamir gestured to a chair. "Sit down, Danny. Did you have breakfast?"

"No," Danny admitted. "I'm too tense from these missions to have much of an appetite."

"Then let's eat," Shamir said, smiling. "Do you like 'sambusak' pastry?"

"Of course," Danny replied. "My mom makes the best 'sambusak' with chickpea filling."

"Great. Bring us two hot 'sambusaks' from 'AbuLafia' in Jaffa. That's your mission for today."

Danny hesitated. He'd never performed a task under direct supervision, let alone with the Head of the Mossad watching. Anxiety bubbled in his chest.

"Focus," Danny told himself. "You've done far more dangerous things in the army. This is nothing."

Closing his eyes, Danny visualized the stand on Yefet Street in Jaffa. His unique ability allowed him to manipulate time in ways others couldn't perceive, but he still felt the weight of the task.

When he opened his eyes, he was holding two hot sambusaks. He placed them on Shamir's desk.

"I need to go back and pay for these," Danny said. "Otherwise, it's stealing."

Shamir raised an eyebrow and then laughed. "I appreciate your honesty," he said. "I'll send someone to pay extra for them later. Now, enjoy—eat while they're hot."

The training continued over the next weeks. Danny undertook increasingly complex challenges: snapping selfies in London, Paris, and New York all in a single day, retrieving classified documents from secure offices, and even entering the office of Israel's Chief of Staff to discreetly remove papers from his desk. Despite a few hiccups, he completed each mission with growing confidence.

A few days later, Danny sat with Professor Wittgenstein. "Shamir wants me to practice 'jumping' into moving cars or trains. I don't know how I can do that."

"You need to divide the jump into two parts," said the Professor. "In the first jump, you jump to a fixed reference point located near the moving object. In the second jump, you already see the target you need to jump to. We know that if you can see the target, your brain can calculate how to reach it even without exact coordinates."

Danny listened and after a few minutes said, "In theory, it's all well and good, but I don't want to find myself in the middle of the highway under the wheels of a truck after missing a moving car."

"We'll need to conduct an experiment under controlled conditions," said Professor Wittgenstein. "I have an idea. I'll talk to Shamir to arrange it."

After several days, Shamir called Danny. "I spoke with the train company CEO. I asked him to keep one empty and closed car for us on tomorrow's ten hundred hours train from Haifa to Tel Aviv. I want you to bring me tomorrow a selfie video of you in the empty car on the section between University Station and 'Savidor' Station in Tel Aviv. The empty car should be the last one."

"Okay," said Danny, "I'll try."

The next day at ten-thirty, Danny and the Professor stood side by side in the control room at Mossad headquarters. Besides them, no one else was in the room.

"According to the schedule, the train should leave University Station at ten-forty and arrive at Savidor Station at ten-forty-five," said the Professor. "You need to jump at ten-forty-two to be sure the train is already in motion, otherwise the experiment won't test your ability to jump into a moving object." Danny nodded.

After a few moments, Danny looked at his watch. The digital display showed ten-forty-one-fifty-five. Danny took deep breaths, looked again at the numbers indicating the coordinates of Tel Aviv University train station, closed his eyes and "jumped."

Professor Wittgenstein estimated that Danny's entire "jump" would take about eighteen seconds. Less than one second for the first jump, about two seconds to zero in on the train's location by sight for executing the second jump into the moving car, and about fifteen seconds to film the video.

After a little more than half a minute, Danny opened his eyes, looked at Professor Wittgenstein with a shocked expression and said: "Only by luck I wasn't run over." Professor Wittgenstein stood astonished. "What happened?"

"I missed the train! That's what happened. In the first 'jump' I reached the platform at University Station. The train had already left the station and was in motion, but I could see it clearly. I 'jumped' again and found myself outside the train, on the parallel track with the train traveling in the opposite direction coming toward me. I jumped into the ditch at the last second. If the train had been one second earlier, it would have crushed me."

Professor Wittgenstein thought for a moment. "I need you to describe exactly where you found yourself in relation to the train you were aiming to jump to. I need to sit down and make calculations and figure out how you can take into account more precisely the speed of motion of the object you want to 'jump' to."

Danny reported the failure to Shamir. "It's not a disaster," said Shamir. "The conclusion is that when planning your operations, we'll need to take into account that you can't 'jump' into a moving object."

The next morning, Shamir said to Danny, "We've played enough, it's time to move up to the big leagues and perform a real operational mission. We know that the Lebanese Hezbollah organization deals in drugs to finance its terrorist activities. Hezbollah is prevented from conducting these transactions itself mainly because no self-respecting international bank agrees to cooperate with a terrorist organization. Therefore, Hezbollah uses Lebanese commercial companies as a cover for its drug business. We suspect that a certain Lebanese company is doing business for Hezbollah through the Swiss bank 'Credit Zurich.'"

"We want to block this possibility, but in order for the Americans to impose sanctions on the Lebanese company and cause all banks in the world to stop working with it, we need evidence. We can break into the bank's computers, but breaching the firewall protecting the bank's servers leaves traces, and we don't want the bank to know that someone breached their computer servers before we have evidence that this Lebanese company is indeed working for Hezbollah."

"What can I do?" asked Danny.

"You'll need to enter the Credit Zurich branch management offices in Zurich, where according to our knowledge the Lebanese company's bank account is managed. We'll equip you with special hardware that can connect directly to the branch manager's terminal and save us the need to overcome the firewall protecting the servers. You'll need to find and copy every document related to the Lebanese company's activities, especially contracts, shipping documents, letters of credit, and the like. In the coming days, you'll undergo an intensive seminar in our intelligence division where they'll teach you how to find and identify the documents, we're interested in."

That week, Danny sat for three days surrounded by dozens of banking and commercial documents, learning how to identify, distinguish, and find the right types of documents.

On Friday, Shamir called Danny and asked, "Are you ready?"

"I'm ready. If I fail, you can fire me and I can go work for a Swiss bank," Danny said with a smile.

"Don't show off," Shamir told him. "Do you know the difference between being smart and being clever?"

"No," said Danny, "what's the difference?"

"The difference is that a clever person easily gets out of trouble that a wise person never gets into in the first place. So don't be a clever guy, and you won't need to get out of trouble you don't need to get into."

"Sorry," said Danny, feeling a bit embarrassed. "The bank will be closed over the weekend. You'll enter the bank on the night between Saturday and Sunday. You'll have enough time to work quietly, find what's needed, copy, and leave without being discovered and without anyone even knowing you were there."

"We'll meet on Saturday night at twenty-two hundred hours in our control room."

On Saturday night exactly at twenty-two hundred hours, Shamir and Danny stood in the control room at Mossad headquarters.

"Are you ready for your first mission?" asked Shamir.

"Yes, yes, of course I'm ready," said Danny, who didn't want to show that he was a bit nervous.

"Go forth, and good luck," said Shamir.

Danny closed his eyes and "jumped."

What Danny didn't know was that Shamir wasn't planning to take any risks. Several weeks before the operation, a well-known international security company had approached Credit Zurich bank's management and offered to perform what's called a "commissioned breach."

In this method, the bank "invites" hackers to try and break into the bank's computers and thereby discover if the bank's defenses are robust or if there are vulnerabilities.

What the bank didn't know was that the security company occasionally works in cooperation with various intelligence organizations and that the "commissioned breach" was intended to ensure that if Danny, on his first mission, was caught by bank security, he would be presented as part of the security company's activities and no one would suspect him of being a Mossad agent.

Danny opened his eyes.

"How was it?" asked Shamir, who didn't want to show Danny that he too was breathing a sigh of relief.

"Everything worked as planned," said Danny and handed

Shamir the special drive with the documents copied from the bank's computers.

"Well done Danny," said Shamir, "go home, see you tomorrow morning."

CHAPTER TEN:
DANNY BECOMES "SCHRÖDINGER"

Danny sat in his office at the "Libertad" unit reading a new study published in the prestigious scientific magazine "Nature" in February 2022. The study dealt with a new material whose developers claimed was stronger than steel but as light as plastic. The researchers claimed that the force needed to deform the new material had to be four times stronger than the force required to penetrate bulletproof glass, and that the material was twice as strong as steel but its chemical structure was much less dense, and it was six times lighter than steel. Danny thought this material could be used to produce strong and durable protective vests and made a note to bring up the idea at the next meeting of Libertad's scientific team.

While Danny was contemplating the possibilities of using the new material, the phone on his desk rang. Due to the secret and confidential nature of work in the Libertad laboratory, it was forbidden to bring in any device capable of transmitting electromagnetic signals of any kind, and all communication was done through encrypted landline phones.

Danny picked up the receiver and answered, "Danny here." "Hello Danny, this is Dina, Shamir's office manager, he'd like to see you for a moment if you have a minute."

Danny knew that if the Head of the Mossad wanted to see him, he needed to get there immediately even if he didn't have a minute. He got up from his chair, left his room, and headed toward the elevator doors that provided access from the underground laboratory to the office floor. The elevator could only be accessed through biometric identification. Danny pressed his finger to the special surface fixed beside the elevator door and said loudly "Danny." The elevator's control system compared the fingerprint and voice print and verified that both belonged to the same person and that this person had authorization to use the elevator, and only then opened the doors. Danny entered the elevator and pressed the button for the top floor. The elevator stopped at the entrance floor and another person whom Danny didn't know entered the elevator. Both went up to the top floor, exited the elevator, and headed toward the Mossad chief's office. Dina, who sat in the reception room, brightened when she saw Danny but first turned to the person who entered with Danny and said to him, "Go in, they're waiting for you."

To Danny she said without using his name: "Sit, they'll call you in a few minutes. Would you like something to drink?"

"Can I have 'yerba mate'?" Danny asked with a smile, the drink he had grown fond of during his South American trip. "It's the famous soccer player Messi's favorite energy drink."

"Danny!!" Dina scolded him with a smile, "The most exotic drink you'll get here is Zero Cola, and even that will probably only be Pepsi."

"But if you ask me out, I'd be happy to have a drink or two with you at my favorite cocktail bar in Tel Aviv." Danny, who wasn't used to this kind of invitation, blushed, coughed, and stammered something about having plans that evening.

The intercom buzzing on Dina's desk saved him. "Go in," she said to him, "they're ready." "But first put this on your face," Dina said and handed him a mask. "Is this a costume party?" asked Danny, "Or did I miss 'Purim'?" "I don't know why they asked you to wear the mask," said Dina, "but you should put it on and go in, they're waiting."

In the room sat three people: the Head of the Mossad, the man who had come up in the elevator with him, and a third person who looked to Danny exactly like the Prime Minister, which amused him slightly.

"Meet 'Schrödinger,'" this is Mr. Gershon Plank, Chairman of the Atomic Energy Committee," the Head of the Mossad pointed to the man who had come up with Danny in the elevator, "and the Prime Minister needs no introduction." "Danny nearly fainted.

"An issue has arisen where we'd like to utilize your special talent," said the Head of the Mossad.

"But before we talk about the matter itself, I want to talk to you about how we deploy you. As you've noticed, you've been with us for almost two years and we haven't asked you to use your abilities. We treat you as a strategic weapon, and a strategic weapon isn't deployed unless it's absolutely vital.

Only we three decide on your deployment: the Prime Minister, Gershon, the Chairman of the Atomic Energy Committee, and myself. Only we three are aware of your existence, and only I know your face and know your name. The other two members know you only by your code name."

"Hello 'Schrödinger,'" said the Prime Minister, "nice to meet a real Israeli superhero. I thank you for your willingness to assist the State of Israel, and I want to assure you that we wouldn't ask you to use your special talent unless we were convinced it was our last option. Good luck to you."

"Thank you," said Danny, and the two men, the Prime Minister and the Chairman of the Atomic Energy Committee stood up. "We'll leave you to discuss the mission details alone," said the Prime Minister, and both left the room.

Danny and Shamir remained alone in the room. "I understand I'm needed," said Danny, "what's this about?"

"We need something from the Archive," said Shamir.

"The Archive? You mean like a repository?"

"Yes, something like that. We need you to bring something from North Korea's government archive."

"Can't you plant a spy there?" asked Danny. "I'm pretty sure we have spies all over the world."

"Let me tell you an old joke that will help you understand the situation," said the Head of the Mossad. "During the Cold War between the United States and the Soviet Union (Russia back then), the Americans tried to plant a perfect spy with the Soviets (that's what we called the Russians then), someone who couldn't be distinguished from a real Russian. After many years of training and preparation, they had a perfect spy. One night, the spy was parachuted near a remote Russian village in the Siberian plains to test if he could blend into Russia as a real Russian. The spy arrived at the village and entered the local tavern. He spent the entire evening and night there. He sang all the Russian songs better than the locals, he danced the 'Kozachok', which is the Russian national dance, better than them, he drank more vodka than anyone else without getting drunk, he told Russian folk tales better than anyone else, and in short, he was a perfect Russian."

"In the morning, it was time to say goodbye to the folks at the tavern. He approached the village head to bid him farewell and saw that his face was grim. 'Is everything alright?' asked the spy, 'Did I do something wrong?' 'You're wonderful,' the village head told him, 'It's just a shame you're a spy.' 'What?' the spy was shocked. 'How did you know I'm a spy?' 'You're African-American,' the village head told him."

"The moral," said the Head of the Mossad to Danny, "is that North Korea is so closed and so unique that even South Koreans, who ethnically belong to the same nation, would immediately stand out as foreigners in North Korea."

"I understand," said Danny, "you need someone who can enter and exit North Korea without being detected at all. And what's in North Korea that's so important to bring?"

"We've learned," said Shamir, "that recently the Iranians have been testing a new ballistic missile called 'Sajil.' This missile, unlike other missiles, is powered by solid fuel and therefore can be launched very quickly without much preparation, and thus cannot be attacked before launch.

This missile can move at a speed of sixteen thousand

kilometers per hour and is therefore very difficult to intercept. The best way is to use electronic warfare measures against it, to disrupt its trajectory and cause it to self-destruct in the air before it reaches Israel's airspace. The great danger of the Sajil missile comes from its ability to carry a nuclear warhead, and that's already a game-changing weapon that we can't allow the Iranians to possess without being sure we know how to prevent it from hitting Israel."

"In order to disrupt the missile's operation, we need to have either the missile itself or the technical specifications according to which the missile was developed, especially its navigation system.

This missile was developed based on North Korean technology; the missile's inertial navigation system is based on North Korean ballistic missiles. We need you to bring us the computer programs embedded in the missile's systems so we can know how to disrupt them.

North Korea's ruler Kim Jong Un is a paranoid who doesn't trust anyone, including his closest family members. Therefore, he keeps all secrets in the national archive, which is his private archive located inside his palace in North Korea's capital, Pyongyang. The American CIA intelligence agency, which is also very interested in understanding exactly what the Iranians have, managed to get information from a North Korean who was formerly part of the ruler's guard team. This person defected from the North to South Korea after he discovered he had fallen out of favor with the ruler because one morning he didn't bow deeply enough to the ruler, which was considered disrespect to the ruler and almost treason against the homeland."

"According to the information provided to us by the Americans, we know that the archive is located in an underground basement beneath the palace. It's a large archive, and we don't know exactly where the ballistic missile diagrams are located. Additionally, we don't want anyone to realize that the archive was breached because then there's a risk the North Koreans will make changes to the navigation systems and all the hard work will be wasted."

"So how will I know exactly which plans I need to find?" asked Danny. "I don't read Korean, and although I'm an engineer, I'm not sure I'll know how to distinguish between navigation system plans and the ruler's kitchen plans."

"In two days, a delegation of Iranian engineers is arriving for a meeting in Pyongyang. We know the purpose of the meeting is to allow the Iranians to study the propulsion and navigation system plans of the Sajil missile. A CIA spy satellite will inform us of the delegation's exact arrival time. You will 'jump' there while the Iranian engineers are in the archive, photograph the diagrams, and disappear."

"Photograph? How? With my cellphone?" asked Danny.

"No," laughed Shamir. "I remind you that you work in the Libertad unit, which is the most advanced technological research unit for espionage equipment. We'll provide you with a special lens for recording video in four-K resolution that will be attached to your retina, will record everything you look at, and will transmit it via Bluetooth technology to a miniaturized memory card that will also be attached to your skull bone right behind your ear."

"Attached how?" Danny asked with concern.

"Don't worry," Shamir told him, "It's a really easy and simple procedure, it'll be like visiting the dentist."

'I hate dentists,' thought Danny, but out loud he said: "When does this happen?" "In five days," said Shamir, "and in the time you have left, you'll learn to use the camera, see some diagrams like the ones you need to photograph so you'll have a good idea what to look for, and you should also refresh your special abilities. We've requested Professor Wittgenstein's help, and he'll meet with you tomorrow at the laboratory."

CHAPTER ELEVEN:
THE ARCHIVE

Danny left the Mossad chief's office. Outside stood Dina, who handed him a sealed envelope. "These are the diagrams you need to review, Amram from the video department will wait for you at two PM for the video equipment installation, and this is for you," she said with a wink and handed him a small note with a phone number.

The camera installation went faster than expected. Danny performed several tests and discovered that once the camera is activated through a dedicated app, he doesn't need to do anything and the camera takes four pictures every second for almost three hours until its battery runs out.

The refresher training with Professor Wittgenstein also proved simple; Danny "jumped" from place to place without difficulty as long as he was given precise coordinates.

"Tomorrow is operation day," Shamir announced to Danny. "I want to make sure you understand the risks and that you're going into this operation wholeheartedly." "I understand and

I'm ready to do whatever is necessary for the state's security," said Danny.

"See you tomorrow," said Shamir.

Danny returned to his rented apartment in Tel Aviv. His heart was heavy. 'This is the first time I'm going on a mission in an enemy country,' he thought, 'perhaps tomorrow I won't return, what will happen to my parents if something happens to me?' He picked up the phone and called his parents' house. His mother answered. "Hello Mom, how are you?" "Everything's fine," said his mother, "how are you? When will we see you? We've barely heard from you since you returned from abroad." "I've been busy," said Danny, "new job and such, you know how it is."

"And why did you call? Did something happen?" "No, no," Danny reassured his mother, "I just wanted to hear your voice. I missed you."

"So come visit, I'll make you the 'Yemenite' soup you love so much."

"Okay Mom, I'll try to come soon. I have to go now, goodbye," he said and hung up.

The day of the operation arrived. In the operation's command post sat the Head of the Mossad, Professor Wittgenstein, and Danny. Danny memorized the target coordinates over and over.

The Head of the Mossad held the phone receiver to his ear; on the other end of the line was the CIA agent sitting in the CIA satellite's control room watching the live feed above the ruler's palace.

"They're reaching the target," said Shamir, "at my command: three, two, one, execute."

Danny remembered the prayer he would recite before every operational activity in the army and whispered quietly, "Hear, O Israel, you are approaching today the battle against your enemies, let not your hearts faint, fear not, nor tremble, neither be afraid of them. For the Lord your God is He that goes with you."

He pressed "play" on the camera app's activation button, put the phone aside, closed his eyes, and focused on the coordinates he had memorized.

Shamir and Professor Wittgenstein watched Danny closely. They saw him close his eyes, his brows furrowing in concentration, and then, almost immediately, he opened them wide.

"It won't work," he said, his voice steady but tinged with frustration. "Only by sheer luck they didn't notice me."

Shamir and the Professor exchanged startled glances. "What's the problem?" Shamir asked, leaning forward in his chair.

Danny took a deep breath. "The room is too crowded. It's small, with a single table in the center, and the diagrams are spread out across it. Four people are huddled around—two Iranians and two North Koreans. I'm worried they'll sense my presence."

"Normally, it's unlikely anyone would sense you," Professor Wittgenstein said thoughtfully, his tone measured. "The speed of your jumps usually prevents detection. But this time, the photography process takes several seconds. That delay could make you vulnerable to being noticed."

"Describe the room to me," Shamir instructed, his mind already working on a solution.

Danny nodded. "It's a basic room, about three meters by four. The walls are bare and painted white. There's a single light bulb hanging from the ceiling above the table. At the far end of the room, there's a simple metal door with a small peephole. No windows—it's in the basement. On the ceiling, near the light bulb, there's a barred opening. It looks like a ventilation duct."

Shamir's eyes lit up. "That's our solution: the ventilation duct. If you jump into it, you can photograph the diagrams from above through the grates. The camera will capture everything you see. If you position yourself just right, you'll get clear shots of the plans."

Professor Wittgenstein frowned. "It's risky. We don't know if the duct is wide enough for a person to fit inside. What if it's too narrow?"

Danny's heartbeat quickened. He felt the familiar tension coursing through his body—the same pulse-pounding adrenaline he'd felt during missions with the Golani reconnaissance unit. He remembered one terrifying encounter near 'Shebaa Farms', when his unit clashed with a terrorist cell. The memory of that chaos, the shock of gunfire, and the anxiety that gripped him afterward rushed back like a wave.

After the battle, his commanders had called him a hero. But Danny only remembered the fear.

He closed his eyes and took a series of deep, calming

breaths. When he opened them, his gaze was steady. "I'm willing to take the risk."

Professor Wittgenstein hesitated. "We'll need to recalculate the coordinates."

"No need," Danny said confidently. "I can do it in two jumps: one into the room, then another into the duct."

Shamir leaned forward, locking eyes with Danny. "Are you sure? Look at me and tell me you're certain."

Danny met his gaze without wavering. "I'm sure."

Shamir nodded firmly. "Go ahead. Get moving before I change my mind."

Danny closed his eyes again, visualizing the coordinates. After a few tense seconds, he reopened them and gave a slight nod.

Shamir turned to the Professor. "Is that it? Did it work?"

Danny answered before Wittgenstein could. "Yes. If the camera functioned as intended, you've got a set of images to analyze."

Shamir wasted no time. "Call Amram from video! Get him here immediately!"

Within moments, Amram burst into the room, slightly out of breath. "Yes, boss? What's going on?"

"Check the photo app on this phone," Shamir instructed, handing over the device. Amram tapped a few icons, opened the gallery, and broke into a grin.

"You've got about sixty images here, boss," he said, holding up the phone.

Shamir allowed himself a rare smile. "Thank you, Amram." He turned to Danny. "How are you feeling?"

Danny shrugged, brushing a hand over his face. "I'm fine. My eye feels a bit irritated from the camera implant, but other than that, no issues."

"Go straight to video and have the camera removed," Shamir instructed. "Then head to the clinic for a full checkup. Tomorrow morning, we'll debrief with the Committee of Three. I need you sharp and alert so we can draw the right lessons from your first operational deployment."

"Thank you, Danny. Now get to the clinic."

Professor Wittgenstein rose from his seat. "I'll go with him. He'll need fluids and sugars to replenish what the jump drained from his system."

Danny waved off the concern. "I'm fine. Besides, Dina promised to take me out for drinks tonight. I'm pretty sure that's better than any IV infusion they'll give me at the clinic."

CHAPTER TWELVE:
OPERATION OPERETTA

The Prime Minister, Defense Minister, IDF Chief of Staff, Head of the Mossad, and Air Force Commander gathered in the Air Force bunker at the Kirya in Tel Aviv.

"Mr. Prime Minister," began the Air Force Commander, "as requested, we've prepared an attack plan for the facility in Shahdad, where the Iranians are developing the nuclear detonator. We have two options.

The first option is to bomb the facility with bunker-buster bombs dropped from aircraft flying directly over it. The advantage of this method is that it guarantees the destruction of the facility. But the downside? Israeli aircraft entering Iranian airspace could easily be considered an act of war."

"And the second option?" the Prime Minister asked.

"The second option is to use long-range missiles. We could deploy 'Popeye Turbo' missiles with 340-kilogram warheads guided by infrared, allowing them to be launched at night. However, the disadvantage is that the warhead's weight is much lighter than a bomb dropped by an aircraft, like a JDAM bomb, which can weigh up to 1,000 kilograms. To make up for this, we'd need pinpoint precision."

"And what's the issue with that?" asked the Prime Minister again.

"There's no issue," the Commander explained, "but we'd need a team from the 'Maglan' unit to parachute near the facility and laser-mark the optimal impact point. This ensures the missiles hit exactly where we need them to."

The Prime Minister frowned, clearly uneasy. "I'm not thrilled about sending Israeli soldiers into the jaws of Iran. If they're caught, it could trigger an all-out war."

"I wouldn't recommend deploying the Maglan unit," the defense minister interjected. "If the Iranians capture Israeli soldiers on their soil, they'll consider it a declaration of war. At that point, we might as well go with the aircraft bombing."

The Chief of Staff stepped forward, spreading out a large map of Iran on the table. "As you can see," he began, "Iran is surrounded by Iraq to the west, the Persian Gulf to the south, Pakistan, Afghanistan, and Turkmenistan to the east, and the Caspian Sea and Azerbaijan to the north. The closest point for launching missiles is the Strait of Hormuz. However, Iran's oil industry in Bandar Abbas is heavily guarded by S-400 surface-to-air missile systems supplied by the Russians. Flying through that region is highly risky, especially since aerial refueling over the Red Sea would be required due to the distance.

"We can't approach over Saudi Arabia or the Gulf emirates, and from the east, the flight path is too long, and the airspace is just as hostile."

The Prime Minister sighed. "If only we had an aircraft carrier in the Indian Ocean. That would solve everything."

"We do have a kind of aircraft carrier," the Chief of Staff replied with a slight smile. "It's called Azerbaijan. Israel and Azerbaijan have excellent security relations, including joint exercises.

"Our plan is for aircraft to take off from the 'Nasosnoye' Air Force base in southeastern Azerbaijan. If we refuel them over the Gorgan Gulf in the southern Caspian Sea, our F-35s could complete a round trip to Shahdad. If direct entry into Iranian airspace isn't approved, we could also launch guided missiles from the same area and return to 'Nasosnoye'."

The Prime Minister nodded, absorbing the information. "I'll convene the cabinet to approve a long-range missile strike from the Gorgan Gulf. In the meantime," he added, turning to the defense minister, "coordinate with the Azeris. Arrange a cover story about a joint rescue exercise. I'll speak with the U.S. President's National Security Advisor to ensure they veto any Iranian attempt to impose sanctions against us in the UN after the attack."

The room fell silent as the Prime Minister concluded, "I want the strike launched within ten days."

Preparations and Launch

The attack mission was assigned to Squadron 140 of the Israeli Air Force, known as the "Golden Eagle" Squadron. The squadron's fleet of F-35 "Adir" stealth aircraft, designed to avoid radar detection, was equipped with two Popeye Turbo missiles under each wing.

At Nasosnoye Air Force base in Azerbaijan, a formation of four aircraft stood ready on the runway.

"Formation One, launch!" commanded the Air Force Commander from the Kirya bunker in Tel Aviv.

"This is Leader One," replied N., the formation commander. "Launching."

One by one, the aircraft roared into the sky, turning south toward the Gorgan Gulf. As they neared the launch point, N. radioed, "Ready for launch."

"Two ready. Three ready. Four ready," the pilots confirmed in sequence.

"Missile launch authorized," the Air Force Commander replied.

"Fire, fire, fire!" N. ordered. Eight missiles detached from the aircraft and plunged downward before their jet engines ignited, propelling them on their 1,000-kilometer journey toward the Shahdad facility.

"Missiles successfully launched," N. reported back.

"Well done," the Air Force Commander said. "Return to base."

The Aftermath

The next morning, the command bunker buzzed with activity. The Head of Military Intelligence (AMAN) approached the Chief of Staff with an update. "We've received satellite data from Ofek-13, our newest and most advanced spy satellite. Despite the Iranians' efforts to conceal the damage, we managed to analyze the excavation levels at the Shahdad facility."

He paused before delivering the bad news. "Our geologists estimate the facility is buried 80 meters underground and protected by a thick reinforced concrete ceiling. Although all eight missiles hit their targets and caused significant damage, the protective dome remained intact. The development laboratories were not destroyed."

The defense minister sighed heavily. "We've failed. All we've done is create a big hole in the ground. The labs are still operational."

The Prime Minister's expression darkened. "I feared this would happen. Time is not on our side. I'll fly to Washington tonight and try to convince the President to help us. The Americans are the only ones with bunker-buster bombs capable of penetrating a facility this deep."

He hesitated. "But without verifying the intel we retrieved from the Supreme Leader's safe; I doubt the President will get Congressional approval for transferring such advanced weapons."

"Who is the source of this intel?" the defense minister asked.

"I can't tell you," The Prime Minister replied. "And frankly, you wouldn't believe me even if I did." He offered a bitter smile. "Just like the President won't."

CHAPTER THIRTEEN:
KRYPTONITE

Three days later, the Prime Minister sat in the secure meeting room where the Committee of Three members met.

"I met with the President of the United States," the Prime Minister reported. "The good news is that he agreed to help us and provide us with missiles with bunker-buster warheads."

"And the bad news?" asked the Chairman of the Atomic Energy Committee.

"The bad news is that he can't get such approval through Congress before the US elections, which means we won't receive the missiles before the end of the year, and that could be too late. That's why I requested this meeting. So we can discuss the possibility of deploying 'Schrödinger' and sending him to sabotage the Iranians' nuclear detonator development laboratory."

"I'm not sure Schrödinger can perform this mission," said the Chairman of the Atomic Energy Committee.

"Why do you say that, Gershon?" wondered the Head of the Mossad.

"When Schrödinger returned from his last mission of breaking into the Supreme Leader's safe, he met with Professor Wittgenstein, and without revealing the exact nature of the mission, he told him that during the break-in he felt something strange. He described it as losing focus, a loss of focus."

"It didn't affect his performance, but Professor Wittgenstein wasn't at ease, and after Danny left, he dedicated thought to the matter and even consulted, without revealing what it was about, with Professor Omer Firstenberg from the Center for Quantum Science and Technology at the Weizmann Institute of Science."

"Following this consultation, Professor Wittgenstein concluded that Schrödinger, like every superhero, might have a 'Kryptonite.'"

"'Kryptonite?'" asked the Prime Minister. "What the hell is 'Kryptonite' and why haven't I heard about this before?"

"That's probably because you're not a comics fan," the Chairman of the Atomic Energy Committee told him. "'Kryptonite' is the material that comes from the fictional planet Krypton where Superman was born, and it's the only material that can weaken him and nullify his superpowers. Since Superman stories were published, the term 'Kryptonite' has become synonymous with what was previously called 'Achilles' heel.'"

"I understand," said the Prime Minister, "we took a beautiful expression from the Iliad and replaced it with children's cartoon nonsense. Indeed, the world is progressing wonderfully toward becoming a paradise of fools."

"In any case," said the Chairman of the Atomic Energy Committee, "it seems Schrödinger is sensitive to some material whose nature we don't yet know, and a small amount of it was probably present in or near the Supreme Leader's safe, and that's probably what caused the loss of focus he reported."

"The concern is that it's isotope 235 of the element uranium which is used in atomic bomb production. Our theory is that there was an item in the safe that was brought from 'Bushehr' where the Iranians produce enriched uranium, and some microscopic particles of isotope 235 stuck to that item and thus reached inside the safe."

"Maybe it happened during the Supreme Leader's last visit to the new centrifuge plant they built last year."

"Our concern is that in the nuclear detonator development laboratory, there's a much larger quantity of this isotope, and we can't know in advance what will happen if Schrödinger is exposed to it."

"So what do we do?" asked the Prime Minister.

"We need to be careful; we need to conduct a series of tests and experiments to verify what really might harm Schrödinger and what dosage might be dangerous for him. After we do that, we'll need to find a way to neutralize the danger."

"How long will that take?" asked the Prime Minister. "We're fighting against time here."

"Several weeks," answered the Chairman of the Atomic Energy Committee.

"We don't have several weeks," ruled the Prime Minister. "You have one week, gentlemen."

"We'll meet tomorrow morning at the laboratory in the Nuclear Research Center in Nahal Sorek," Professor Wittgenstein told Danny and hung up the phone.

The next day, Danny arrived at Professor Wittgenstein's laboratory at the Nuclear Research Center.

"Do you remember the phenomenon you described to me when we last met at my house in Jerusalem?" asked the Professor.

"Yes," said Danny, "I had a feeling of losing focus."

"We think you're sensitive to isotope 235, and I want to check how much it might affect you."

"In the adjacent laboratory, there are six separate chambers, in each of which we've prepared a tiny sample of the suspected material. Each chamber has a slightly larger amount of the material. You'll start with the minimal amount, and if we see it doesn't affect you, you'll move to the next chamber which will have a larger amount, and so on until we know whether the material indeed affects you and in what way."

"I ask that you don't enter the chamber but rather 'jump' into it so that the experiment is conducted under conditions of using your special talent."

"Ready?"

"Ready," said Danny.

"Go ahead, jump to chamber number one."

Danny closed his eyes and immediately opened them again.

"How did you feel?" asked the Professor. "Normal," Danny told him, "Nothing special."

"Try chamber number one again," the Professor told him, "But this time double the relative time you stay in the chamber."

Danny again closed his eyes and opened them again.

"Well?" asked the Professor.

"Nothing," Danny told him.

"Okay, let's move to chamber number two."

Danny jumped and returned. "I didn't feel anything," he said.

"Double the time again," said the Professor.

Danny jumped again and returned. "Nothing," he said to the Professor.

What Danny didn't know was that the Professor had to verify that what Danny felt during the safe operation wasn't something psychological but rather a real physical phenomenon. Therefore, in chambers one and two, there wasn't any trace of isotope 235.

If Danny had felt strange in either of these chambers, the Professor would have known that Danny's sensation wasn't physical but psychological, and therefore needed to be treated by different means.

"Ready for chamber number three?" asked the Professor, knowing that this time Danny would be exposed to the dangerous material.

"Ready," answered Danny.

Danny jumped… To the Professor, it seemed like an hour had passed, but after a second, Danny opened his eyes.

"Dizziness," he said. "I felt double and I also had some dizziness."

"That's your 'Kryptonite,'" the Professor told him, "you can't be exposed to uranium isotope 235, it could harm you."

Danny, as a materials engineer, immediately understood what this meant. "So what do we do?" he asked practically.

"We don't do anything," said the Professor, "I do, and you go rest. Go home, I saw that nice girl from Shamir's office looking at you. Call her, go to a movie together or take a walk on the beach, rest, and I'll call you the moment I know something useful."

After Danny left his house, Professor Wittgenstein called his friend Professor Yitzhak Ben-Israel from the Chemical Physics Department at Tel Aviv University.

"I can't give too many details and explain why I'm asking, but I need to find a quick way to get rid of isotope 235," Professor Wittgenstein said.

"It's very simple," laughed Professor Ben-Israel. "Uranium in nature has only three isotopes. These isotopes differ from each other only in the number of 'neutrons' in their atom's nucleus: the isotopes are: uranium two 238, 235, and 234 Of these three, only 235 is fissile material, meaning it can be used to produce a nuclear bomb working on the principle of atomic fission. If you find a way to remove a neutron or add a neutron to an atom of isotope 235, it won't be 235 anymore but something else."

"The difference between uranium 235 and uranium 234 is

just one neutron. If you find a way to get rid of one neutron, then you've solved your problem and, by the way, you'll probably get a Nobel Prize in Physics." Professor Ben-Israel burst out laughing.

"This isn't funny," Professor Wittgenstein said angrily, "this is an urgent problem that needs a quick solution."

"Maybe if you explain the problem a bit better to me, I can give you more practical advice and not just a chemistry lesson."

"Hmm," said Professor Wittgenstein, "the problem is that I want to prevent exposure to isotope 235."

"Then don't hang around uranium enrichment centrifuges or nuclear reactors," said his friend, suppressing his smile.

"And if I must be there?" said Wittgenstein.

"Then protect yourself," Professor Ben-Israel told him. "Wear a protective suit coated with 'neutron-absorbing' materials. Any contact of the isotope with this suit will change the atomic composition of the isotope and the problem is solved."

"'Neutron-absorbing' materials?" asked the Professor. "Like 'dysprosium'? You probably know that the name 'dysprosium' comes from the Greek word 'dyspositos' which means 'hard to get.' Where will I find a material, whose name means 'hard to get'?"

"That's actually not a problem," said Ben-Israel, "everyone who works with lasers uses dysprosium."

"Thank you," said Professor Wittgenstein, "you've helped me a lot."

"My pleasure," said Professor Ben-Israel and hung up the phone, scratching his forehead curiously.

"'Dysprosium'?" asked Gershon Plank, Chairman of the Atomic Energy Committee.

"Yes, and a lot of it," answered Professor Wittgenstein. "We have four days to produce and test a radioactivity-protection suit coated with dysprosium."

"The lucky thing is that we have a materials engineer who can participate in the production and testing without us having to explain to someone from outside why on earth we need such a thing."

"I'll talk immediately with the Prime Minister to direct the Defense Ministry to locate, collect, and transfer to us all the necessary quantity without asking questions and without paperwork and bureaucracy."

Professor Wittgenstein called Danny and asked him to come to Nahal Sorek immediately.

"But I made a date with Dina," said Danny, who hadn't yet found the courage to call Dina and ask her on a date but was looking for an excuse.

"Don't confuse me," said the Professor, "we need to start working on your 'Kryptonite,' time is short and there's much work to be done."

"Okay," said Danny, feeling a bit happy to have an excuse not to make a call that made him a bit nervous, "half an hour and I'll be with you." The Professor explained the mission to Danny. "No one can manage to develop and produce a protective suit that also needs to be coated with material made from a rare element and manage to test it within ninety-six hours," said Danny.

"You're wrong," the Chairman of the Atomic Energy Committee told him, "There is one organization that can."

"Which organization?" wondered Danny.

"You know Q, the scientist who supplies James Bond with all the most imaginative technological gadgets there are?"

"Yes, of course I know, who hasn't seen Q in James Bond movies."

"Well, we have our own Q."

"We do?" Danny was surprised.

"Yes, Unit 81," said the Chairman of the Atomic Energy Committee.

"Unit 81, or by its full name 'The Technological Unit of the Special Operations Division' is a unit in the Special Operations Division under the IDF Intelligence Division that deals with providing technological solutions for operational needs of the Intelligence Division. The unit specializes in rapid development of unique tools and technologies especially for use in classified intelligence operations beyond the border."

"Tonight, the unit's engineers will receive a shipment of dysprosium that will be sent by order of the Defense Ministry from the warehouses of the defense companies 'Rafael' and 'Elbit'."

"Tomorrow morning you will report there with the cover story of being the Mossad's materials engineer, and together with them you will develop, produce, and test this crazy suit."

"What's so urgent?" wondered Danny, who wasn't at all

privy to the plan to send him on a top-secret mission deep into Iran to neutralize the nuclear detonator threat.

"You're going on a new 'mission,'" the Head of the Mossad told him, who had meanwhile arrived and joined the conversation. "You'll receive a full briefing immediately after we're sure you can overcome your 'Kryptonite.'"

Danny and the unit's engineers worked continuously for forty-eight hours without a break. There were dozens of obstacles that needed to be overcome: they needed to find a way to turn the dysprosium into spray, they needed to overcome the fact that the material tended to evaporate quickly, and they needed to find a way to stabilize it.

Danny sat for hours in front of the computer reading countless international studies about this rare element and about the various possibilities to handle and utilize it, and Unit 81 engineers tried again and again different and strange ideas, some genius and some really foolish.

After forty-eight hours, they had one suit ready for testing. Danny took the suit and drove quickly to the Nuclear Research Center where Professor Wittgenstein was waiting for him anxiously.

"This time we won't waste time on empty chambers," said the Professor. "Put on the suit and jump immediately to chamber number three where you felt the symptoms from exposure to isotope 235 that's dangerous to you." He looked at Danny as he said these last words.

Danny put on the suit. He closed his eyes. And after several seconds opened his eyes.

"It's not working," he said to the Professor, "I felt dizzy

again. Maybe we should forget about this whole suit business and I'll take the risk."

"Are you crazy?" Professor Wittgenstein shouted, "In chamber number three there was a tiny amount of this isotope. There's no telling what will happen if you're exposed to a large amount. We're talking about a nuclear laboratory; you could die or worse - get stuck there and fall into Iranian hands."

"You know we have no choice," said Danny. "If the matter is so critical and urgent then I'll have to take the risk."

The next morning, the Head of the Mossad called for Danny. "I understand we haven't succeeded in overcoming the 'Kryptonite.' In light of this, and due to the magnitude of the threat and its urgency, the Prime Minister has authorized executing the operation with the knowledge that you might be exposed to the dangerous isotope and get hurt.

Ron Sarig

CHAPTER FOURTEEN:
OPERATION ELUL

"We tried to destroy the nuclear detonator development lab in Shahdad, but we failed," the Head of the Mossad said grimly.

Danny's expression remained calm, even as the weight of the words hung in the air.

"I know this mission is extraordinarily dangerous," the Mossad chief continued. "But we wouldn't ask you to take on such a risk if it weren't critical to the survival of Israel. The stakes couldn't be higher."

Danny nodded, a faint smirk forming on his lips. "I didn't get these powers to skip the line for the Black Mamba at Disneyland," he said. "Let's do this."

The Mossad chief allowed himself a brief smile before resuming his serious tone. "This mission is unlike anything you've done before. It's not about stealing documents or breaking into a safe. This time, you'll be planting an explosive device—a small but extremely powerful bomb—inside the nuclear detonator development lab. Your objective is to ensure the entire underground facility is destroyed. This is a follow-up to Operation Operetta, which didn't get the job done."

Danny's jaw tightened as he listened.

"One more thing," the Mossad chief said. "If something goes wrong, we can't extract you. Any military incursion into Iranian territory or airspace could spark a war, and we're not prepared to go that far. If your 'Kryptonite' weakens you and you're captured, you'll be on your own."

"Understood," Danny replied, his voice steady.

The next day at noon, Danny reported to the Mossad chief's office. "I've practiced planting and activating the bomb dozens of times," he said. "I can disassemble and reassemble it blindfolded. I'm ready."

"The operation is set for tonight at 1:30 AM, Tehran time. At that hour, only guards will be outside the facility. The lab itself should be empty, giving you time to plant the bomb without interference. Return here at midnight for a final briefing. Until then, rest, clear your head, and don't think about Iranians or uranium."

Danny nodded and left the office, only to find Dina, the office manager, waiting for him.

"I've been waiting for you to call me," she said, crossing her arms. "But I see that if I don't take matters into my own hands, we'll both be retired before you work up the nerve. So, I reserved us a table at the Imperial cocktail bar tonight at eight. Don't be late."

Danny opened his mouth to respond but could only manage an awkward squeak. He nodded quickly and hurried away; his face flushed.

At eight o'clock, Danny and Dina were seated in the elegant Imperial Bar on 'Hayarkon' Street in Tel Aviv.

"What would you like to drink?" the waiter asked.

"Do you have Fanta?" Danny asked innocently.

Dina rolled her eyes, laughing. "He's joking," she told the waiter. "Two mojitos, please."

When the drinks arrived, Dina raised her glass. "Cheers," she said.

"Cheers," Danny replied, taking a sip. Almost immediately, he began coughing uncontrollably.

"It's... strong," Danny managed to say between coughs.

Dina laughed so hard she had to put her drink down. "You're the cutest nerd I've ever met. How did you survive 'Golani' with this level of niceness?"

Danny smiled sheepishly. "We were a 'Bnei Yeshiva' platoon," he said. "Everyone was nerdy."

"Bnei Yeshiva? You studied at a yeshiva?" Dina asked.

"Yeah," Danny said. "Amit High School Yeshiva in Ashdod."

"Now everything makes sense," Dina said with a teasing grin. "Why don't you wear a kippah? Did you become secular?"

"It's complicated," Danny replied. "Let's just say I'm strong in faith but not strict about all six hundred and thirteen commandments."

The two spent the next two hours sharing stories about their childhoods and dreams for the future.

"What do you want to do when you grow up?" Dina asked.

Danny hesitated. He couldn't tell her that by the next morning, he might be in Iranian custody—or worse. "It's late," he said instead. "I have a project to prepare for tomorrow. I should head back to the office."

"Workaholics," Dina sighed. "Fine. But don't you dare not call me tomorrow night." Danny smiled and promised he would before heading back to the Mossad offices.

By 11:25 PM, Masked Danny, the Prime Minister, the Chairman of the Atomic Energy Committee, and the Head of the Mossad were gathered in the control room for the final briefing.

"Let's review the mission details one last time," the Mossad chief said.

"I enter the facility, locate the nuclear detonator, attach the explosive device, set it to detonate, and get out," Danny recited.

"Exactly. Here are the coordinates," the Mossad chief said. "Go. And may God protect you."

Danny closed his eyes.

Five seconds passed. Ten seconds. Twenty. Danny stood motionless; his eyes shut tight.

"Is it always like this?" the Prime Minister asked nervously.

"No," the Mossad chief replied, frowning.

Thirty seconds passed.

"I'm afraid we've lost him," the Mossad chief muttered. "The Kryptonite must have affected him."

Before anyone could respond, Danny's eyes flew open.

"It's not there," he said breathlessly.

"What's not there?" the Prime Minister demanded.

"The nuclear detonator. It's gone."

"Are you sure?" asked the Chairman of the Atomic Energy Committee.

"I searched everywhere. I was there for almost two hours. The lab was completely empty."

"Two hours?" the Prime Minister asked, turning to the Mossad chief. "What happened to him? Is he still thinking straight?"

"Two hours on relative time," the Mossad chief explained.

"Relative schmalative," the Prime Minister snapped. "Find out where that detonator went, and fast."

As the Prime Minister stormed out, the Mossad chief turned to Danny. "Are you okay?"

"I'm fine," Danny said. "Exhausted and starving, but fine."

"Go to the clinic for a checkup," the Mossad chief instructed. "We'll order you a pizza. What toppings do you want?"

"Mushrooms," Danny said with a small smile.

"Eat, rest, and be back here at ten tomorrow morning for a full debrief."

Danny nodded, his mind already racing. The detonator was gone, and he had a sinking feeling the mission was far from over.

Ron Sarig

CHAPTER FIFTEEN:
THE NUCLEAR DETONATOR

"How could you miss this?" shouted the Prime Minister.

"Right after the bombing that failed in Operation Operetta, the Iranians realized we were onto them and removed the detonator from there and moved it to another location," said the Head of Military Intelligence.

"They're smart, they took advantage of a cloudy night and covered the trucks with sheets that don't reflect infrared, so our satellites couldn't detect it."

"So we have no idea where the detonator is now?" asked the Prime Minister.

"You can only leave 'Shahdad' in two directions, south toward Bandar Abbas or north toward central Iran," said the Head of Military Intelligence. "The Americans have more 'eyes' on that area, and we've asked them to go back and check their footage to see if they saw a convoy traveling on either of these roads in the two days after the bombing in Operation Operetta."

"We're waiting for an answer, hoping they'll give us a lead that will allow us to discover where they've hidden the detonator."

"I have a guess," said Shamir. "To minimize the detonator's exposure to an air strike, the Iranians needed to find a new location as close as possible to 'Shahdad.' They couldn't risk the detonator on a long journey to their nuclear facilities in the Isfahan area, which is nine hundred kilometers from 'Shahdad.'"

"I also don't believe they prepared another underground bunker in advance just in case the detonator development laboratory's location would be discovered and force them to hide the detonator in a new location."

"Therefore, I think they hid the detonator in the closest possible place to Shahdad."

"I'm betting the detonator is now hidden in the Iranian nuclear facility 'Lavisan' northeast of Tehran. 'Lavisan' is only five hundred kilometers from 'Shahdad,' and they could make the entire journey in one night." It's a nuclear facility that Iran has never declared, and it's perfect for them as a hiding place for the detonator."

"First, ask the Americans to check if they had satellite coverage over the road there during the two nights after the attack, and whether there really was a convoy traveling there that left 'Shahdad.' Besides that, activate every agent, every information source, and every collaborator you have in Iran," said the Prime Minister. "We must find this detonator and quickly."

Meanwhile, at the Nuclear Research Center in Nahal Sorek, Professor Wittgenstein sat racking his brain about how to solve the 'Kryptonite' problem.

He knew that Danny had volunteered to perform the mission without protection and was relieved that Danny wasn't exposed to the dangerous isotope 235 during the break-in at 'Shahdad.'

"I must understand why our idea didn't work," thought the Professor. "We did everything by the book."

He called his friend Professor Ben-Israel from the Physical Chemistry Department at Tel Aviv University again and told him in general terms about the attempt to use dysprosium and about the failure.

"You're right, your idea to use dysprosium was smart and should have worked on paper."

"But to help you, I need a bit more information to understand what happened," Professor Ben-Israel told him.

"Send me all the data and formulas you used to prepare the material, and I'll run a test here and try to understand what the problem is."

"I can't send you the data, it's classified information and I can't let it circulate around the country like that. Come here, it's important and also urgent."

"I have a faculty meeting at four PM, I'll finish it and come to you."

In the early evening at six-thirty pm, the two professors sat in the laboratory and reviewed the failed experiment data.

"I think I know what the problem is," said Professor Ben-Israel. "Uranium, like all heavy elements, is not chemically stable. In the atom's nucleus of heavy elements, a process called decay is constantly occurring."

"Decay is actually the process of atom decomposition. The by-product of the decomposition is radioactive radiation."

"The problem isn't with the dysprosium element, it's doing its job. The problem is that in the process where you turned the dysprosium into spray, you added a material that has an extra neutron in its atom nucleus. What happened is that isotope 235 lost a neutron to the dysprosium and received in return a neutron from the material that turned the dysprosium into spray, and in total the number of neutrons in the isotope didn't change, and therefore you didn't achieve the desired result."

Professor Wittgenstein nodded in understanding.

"What you need to do is find another material to turn the dysprosium into spray, or alternatively, you need to change the electrical polarity of the protective suit, which will change its electrical valence and prevent the unwanted change."

"I understand," said Professor Wittgenstein, "thank you very much, you've helped me and the people of Israel greatly."

Professor Wittgenstein called Danny and said to him, "Go immediately to Unit 81, tell them they need to find a way to polarize the protective suit so it won't lose a neutron in the reaction with isotope 235."

"I'm preparing the chambers for a repeat test. Come here the moment you have a ready suit."

Danny drove immediately to the camp where Unit 81 was located and explained the necessary change to the unit's chief engineer.

"It'll take me an hour, wait here," the engineer told him. "I think I have a simple idea how to make the change you're requesting."

After an hour, the engineer returned to Danny, who sat biting his nails in the waiting room. "Here you go," he said to Danny, "here's the upgraded suit."

"So fast?" asked Danny, "What change did you make?"

"A small change," said the chief engineer. "We added two thin copper wires in the suit's belt and connected them to a six-volt battery that costs half a dollar, and added an on/off switch for the battery."

"The moment you press the power button, the battery will send a low-intensity electrical current through the copper wires we added to the suit, and there you have a perfectly polarized suit."

Danny thanked him, took the suit, got into his car, and raced toward the Nuclear Research Center in Nahal Sorek where Professor Wittgenstein was waiting for him to repeat the experiment.

He repeated to the Professor the explanation he received from the chief engineer regarding the upgrade made to the suit.

"Go ahead," said the Professor, "the test chambers are ready, start with chamber number three."

Danny put on the protective suit, pressed the button

activating the small battery connected to the suit's belts, and walked toward chamber number three.

"Wait, wait," the Professor stopped him, "don't enter on foot, 'jump' into the chamber like you would in the real operation."

Danny closed his eyes and after ten long seconds opened them again.

"Well?" the Professor asked tensely.

"Nothing! All good, no dizziness and I was in full focus in all the chambers."

"What do you mean in all the chambers?" asked the Professor. "You were only in chamber number three."

"No," laughed Danny, "when I understood I was feeling good in chamber number three, I decided to jump directly to chamber number four and so on to five and six."

Professor Wittgenstein opened his eyes wide and looked at Danny as if looking at a madman, and then burst into great laughter, hugged Danny and shouted "We succeeded! We succeeded! I was already sure I was going to lose you, you madman."

Danny took the suit and drove straight to Mossad headquarters in north Tel Aviv. He entered his office and called the Head of the Mossad's office. Dina answered the phone. "I need to talk to the boss," said Danny.

"Hello Danny," Dina said with a smile, "how good that you're calling me, I hope you had fun yesterday," she told him with a smile.

"Ah, yes, no," Danny got confused.

"So you didn't enjoy?" Dina laughed.

"No, yes, of course, it was fun," Danny stammered.

"So you're probably calling to ask me out again," said Dina.

"Uh.....no."

"No??" asked Dina, "You don't want to go out with me again?"

"Yes, yes of course I want to," Danny blurted out, "but that's not why I called, I need to report to the boss."

"Then come up here," said Dina and laughed, "he's waiting for you."

Danny entered Shamir's office.

"We've overcome the 'Kryptonite' problem," he reported happily to the Head of the Mossad.

"Really? I'd completely forgotten about that. We have a bigger problem."

"Am I allowed to know what the problem is?" asked Danny.

"We don't know where the nuclear detonator is," answered Shamir.

"That is indeed a problem," Danny admitted with a fallen face. "Can I help with anything?"

"Only if you have a time machine to go back to the night they moved the detonator from 'Shahdad' to another place so you could track it," said Shamir.

"I don't have a time machine," admitted Danny, "but I know who does."

"What do you mean?" asked Shamir.

"If the Iranians installed surveillance cameras at

intersections for security purposes, maybe I can 'jump' to visit their control center and check the recordings from those nights that interest us. That could at least give us a lead on where to start looking."

"That's an interesting idea," said Shamir, "very interesting... Thank you, Danny, you're dismissed."

Danny left Shamir's office and heard him shouting to Dina, "Tell Gil from Cyber to come up here immediately."

"I heard you're dismissed," said Dina to Danny, "want to go get something to eat together?"

"I would really love to go eat with you together," said Danny with rare courage, "but the truth is I'm completely exhausted from all the running around and I'm not sure I'll have the energy to eat now, and I also need to catch a few hours of sleep."

"Well," Dina said disappointedly, "if you don't want to, you don't have to."

"We'll go tomorrow," said Danny, "I promise."

"I'll consider it," said Dina with a smile, "drive home and go to sleep. We'll talk tomorrow."

As Danny was leaving, Gil from Cyber was standing at the door. "What does the boss want from me at this hour?" he whispered to Dina.

Dina shrugged her shoulders, "I have no idea, go in and see."

Gil entered Shamir's office. "

I need you to obtain traffic camera recordings," Shamir said to him. "No problem, boss. Whose recordings?" Gil asked. "Did you run a red light and need to destroy evidence so you won't get a traffic ticket?"

"No way," Shamir replied, "I need the traffic cameras of the Iranians." "The Iranians??" Gil was stunned.

"Yes," Shamir told him, "I need you and your hackers to break into the Iranian traffic control center and find me footage from these two nights," he said, throwing him a slip of paper with the requested dates. "Iran is a huge country," Gil said to him, "can you narrow down the area for me a bit?"

"Yes," Shamir replied, "start with 'Shahdad' and search cameras within a 500-kilometer radius. Dump everything you find to the decoding department. I'll tell them what to look for."

And on the way out, tell Dina to get Zohar from the Intelligence Management and Ram from the 'Neviot' Unit on the phone.

The next morning at ten o'clock, the head of the Mossad called the Prime Minister on the encrypted phone, "We found the lost package," he informed him. "Excellent," the Prime Minister said, "You can be an excellent lost and found department. When are you sending someone to 'pick up' the package?" "I think we'll do it tonight," Shamir told him.

Ron Sarig

CHAPTER SIXTEEN:
OPERATION ELUL RETURNS

The Committee of Three sat in the offices of the government Company on the Mediterranean Coast.

We discovered that, as we suspected, the Iranians indeed hid the nuclear detonator at their facility in "Lavisan".

This complex is much larger than the one in "Shahdad" and therefore there is no point in attacking it from the air because we have no idea which point to bomb. For the same reason, we cannot give "Schrödinger" precise coordinates, and I do not see him wandering around a secured nuclear facility asking people exactly where the nuclear detonator is hidden.

So, what is the plan? asked the Prime Minister.

We will need to make the Iranians take out the nuclear detonator and then strike it, said Shamir.

And exactly how will we do that? asked Gershon, chairman of the Nuclear Energy Committee.

We will make them think we have discovered the hiding place of the nuclear detonator. The moment the Iranians think we know where the detonator is hidden, they will fear we will hit it and try to transfer it to another location. This time we will know in advance that this is what they are planning to do, and we will track them closely, discover when the convoy carrying the detonator leaves for the new hiding place, and then when the nuclear detonator is moving on a truck on an open road, we will be able to attack and destroy it.

And how do you plan to make the Iranians understand that we know where the nuclear detonator is hidden? asked the Prime Minister.

We will send "Schrödinger" to create chaos in the facility. Maybe we will plant a bomb or steal documents from the safes in a way that leaves traces. The moment they discover that someone infiltrated the facility and tried to sabotage it or conducted a search aimed at finding something important, this will trigger a red light for them and cause them to try to transfer the nuclear detonator to another location.

And how will we hit the detonator?

The facility is relatively close to the Caspian Sea, only three hundred kilometers separate the facility's location from where we launched the missiles in Operation Operetta. The proximity will allow the Air Force to equip planes with much heavier missiles. Once we receive a satellite image of the convoy, we can give the Air Force precise coordinates and say goodbye to the nuclear detonator.

And when will you send "Schrödinger" to create the chaos, as you put it? asked the Prime Minister.

The plan is to carry out the infiltration tonight, Shamir answered.

The infiltration will only be discovered near dawn, which will give the Air Force time to prepare a squadron that will leave tonight to the Azerbaijani Air Force base in "Nasosnaiya". From there, the squadron can maintain a presence for forty-eight hours, with each pair of planes armed with air-to-ground missiles. These missiles will be launched at targets broadcast from the Air Force's "bunker" directly to the firing computers of the planes the moment the satellite locates the convoy with the nuclear detonator.

So, you will send Schrödinger tonight, said the Prime Minister. I will convene an urgent cabinet meeting and report to the ministers, and afterward we will meet in the "bunker" in the Kirya with the Chief of Staff, Air Force Commander, and Head of Intelligence and brief them about the part they are allowed to know in order to execute the mission.

At exactly one-thirty after midnight, the Head of the Mossad and Danny stood in the command room at Mossad headquarters.

Aside from them, no one else was in the room.

I want you to enter the offices in the "Lavisan" facility and create a bit of chaos, they both looked at the aerial photo (photographed by the Ofek-13 satellite the night before).

These are the facility's offices, and this is the operational area with fuel tanks that feed the facility's generators, the Head of Mossad pointed to the buildings.

I want you to steal some documents from the facility's offices. It does not really matter which documents, the main thing is to leave signs of theft, throw some papers on the floor and leave drawers open.

Then plant these near the fuel tanks, he said and handed Danny two seemingly innocent boxes.

These are two small explosive charges that the technology department prepared specifically for cases where you need to make a lot of noise. You set the timer to thirty minutes, press the green button, plant the charges under the tanks and leave with the documents you have stolen.

Ready? the Head of Mossad asked. Did you memorize the coordinates? Remember you have two reference points tonight, first the offices and then the fuel tanks.

Ready, said Danny.

Go ahead. And good luck.

Danny pressed the activation button for the battery that supplies electricity to the protective suit, verified that the light indicating the battery was operating glowed red, closed his eyes, and ten seconds later opened them again.

Done! he reported to the Head of Mossad and handed him a pile of documents filled with complicated-looking diagrams in Farsi.

And the charges? asked the Head of Mossad. Planted exactly as you instructed, said Danny.

Let us see what you did, said the Head of Mossad and turned to the television screen broadcasting an image from the control screen in the Intelligence Directorate's satellite unit.

After twenty-nine minutes, a small spark of fire was seen,

and immediately afterward two large fireballs appeared in the center of the picture.

The Head of Mossad called the Prime Minister on the encrypted line. The bait is in place, he reported.

We will wait and see if the fish take the bait, said the Prime Minister and hung up the phone.

The next evening, two fighter jets of the F-35 model circled above the southern Caspian Sea, tense and waiting for the order to launch seemingly malicious air-to-ground missiles, directly to the targets that would be transmitted immediately to the firing computers of the planes as soon as the convoy carrying the nuclear detonator to a new hiding place is revealed.

In the Air Force's "bunker," an operations officer stood with a phone to his ear, on the other end was the controller watching the satellite image, alert to any movement at the "Lavisan" facility.

"I see truck movement," the controller reported.

"Follow them and give me their precise coordinates the moment the convoy leaves the civilian-populated area," said the Air Force operations officer.

"Roger," the controller responded, "stay on the line."

"Of course, I will stay on the line, where else would I go now, to a Pilates class?" the operations officer muttered to himself.

"I see movement of a large number of vehicles," the controller updated from the satellite image. "They are leaving the facility and moving towards the nearby interchange that leads to highways outside the district. They have reached the interchange, wait… we have a problem," the controller shouted.

"What problem?" asked the operations officer.

"They have split into three different convoys, each taking an exit from the interchange in a different direction," said the controller. "I do not know which convoy to track."

"Wait for further instructions," said the operations officer and turned to the Air Force Commander, who already had the encrypted phone in his hand.

"Are you hearing this, Shamir?" the Air Force Commander said to the Head of the Mossad on the other end of the phone.

"Hearing," said Shamir.

"We have a problem. The Iranians are smarter than we assumed. They realized this could be a trap and split the convoy into three different convoys, each heading to a different place. We do not have three satellites to track all three convoys, and even if we wanted to attack all three, we could only track one."

"So, we have four possible targets and we can only know the location of two," said the Head of the Mossad.

"Why four?" asked the Air Force Commander. "The report we received was that they split into three."

"True," said Shamir, "but what if they are outsmarting us and all three are a decoy, and they have actually left the nuclear detonator in the facility?"

"From our perspective, we could bomb all the convoys and believe we have eliminated the threat, but what would really happen is they would complete the detonator installation, and we would be screwed, as the guys say."

"So, what do you propose?" asked the Air Force Commander.

"I have an idea," said Shamir. "Give me an hour."

Shamir hung up the phone and asked Dina to get Professor Wittgenstein on the phone.

"Good evening, Head of Mossad," said Professor Wittgenstein in the drowsy voice of someone awakened from deep sleep. "How can an old scientist help you?"

"I have a question about the young man you raised," said Shamir.

"What is the question?"

"Until now, we have 'jumped' him to a single target each time."

"Yes, and what of it?" asked the Professor.

"Can he do multiple deliveries at the same time?"

"He can do more deliveries than a DoorDash delivery driver does in a year," laughed the Professor. "He is like 'Amazon'."

"I understand," said Shamir, "thank you very much and good night."

"Call Danny and tell him to come here immediately," Shamir told Dina.

"Immediately?" asked Dina. "He is probably at home. It will take at least half an hour."

"Tell him I requested he come immediately," said Shamir, "tell him I said he needs to jump here right away. I have a feeling he is not far from here." He added that he did not want to start explaining things to Dina that he should not explain.

Dina called Danny, who was sleeping in his rented apartment in Tel Aviv. "The boss wants you here immediately."

"Immediately?" asked Danny. "How?"

"I told him it would take you at least half an hour," said Dina, "but he said to tell you to jump here right away, and he has a feeling you are not far from here."

"I understand," said Danny. "Tell him we will meet in the usual command room in five minutes."

"In five minutes?" Dina was stunned. "But how?"

"Never mind," said Danny. "I am really close to you."

Five minutes later, Danny appeared in the command room at Mossad headquarters.

Shamir stood in the control room talking on the phone: "Are you still seeing all three convoys?" he asked the listener on the other end. "Yes? Good. In how long will they exit your range?" A pause. "Six to seven minutes at most? I understand. Please calculate where they will be in five minutes and send me their coordinates immediately," he said and hung up.

He took three small devices from the table and gave them to Danny.

"These are homing beacons," he said. "The moment they are activated, they send their location every ten seconds in an encrypted radio burst on a frequency known to us. The location is sent to the firing computers of the 'Popeye' missiles installed under the F-35 aircraft wings.

"These missiles have an inertial navigation system and will know how to correct their trajectory to reach the target even if the target is moving.

"Bring the protective suit," Shamir told him, "And learn the coordinates that will appear on the screen in a moment."

"I need you to visit them all simultaneously. Do not waste time checking whether the nuclear detonator is in one of the convoys. Stick a homing beacon on one truck from each convoy, verify it is active, and return here immediately."

Danny looked at the screen and memorized the coordinates that appeared.

He remembered that to crack the safe's code, he had split into multiple appearances, but in fact they were all in the same place. He had never jumped simultaneously to multiple different coordinate points.

He wanted to call Professor Wittgenstein to confirm that he could "jump" simultaneously to three different targets, each located on a moving truck. He remembered clearly that the last time he tried to jump onto a moving body, the train almost ran him over.

Danny took a deep breath. "I need to take the truck's speed into account," he thought. He remembered the example Professor Wittgenstein gave him after the "jump" failure to the moving train. "Remember your military shooting training," the Professor had told him then. How do you hit a moving target?

Danny remembered that if you aim the shot where the target is currently located, the shot will miss the target because the bullet takes between one and two milliseconds to reach the target, and meanwhile the target moves. Therefore, to hit a moving target, you shoot slightly ahead, aiming so the bullet will hit where the target will be when the bullet reaches it.

"Exactly," the Professor told him. "Take into account the

movement speed of your target, and 'jump' to where it will be in a second, not where it is now. Our brain can easily estimate the distance."

Danny started to tell Shamir "I cannot...," but the look on Shamir's face left no room for doubt. It was now or never.

Danny checked that the "anti-kryptonite" suit was fastened tightly, activated the electrical polarity battery, held the three homing beacons, said "Shema Yisrael" and "jumped," and jumped, and "jumped".

Shamir called the Air Force Commander again, who was sitting in the "bunker" in the Kirya.

"We found a way to place homing beacons on the convoys," he told him.

"The homing beacons will broadcast for the next four hours and allow us to know the convoy's location at any time, even without a satellite. This will give you enough time to get more planes in the air.

"In a few moments, three different coordinate points will be sent to the Air Force control center and the planes' firing computers. Raise two more pairs of F-35 aircraft so that each pair attacks a different convoy. This will give us four missiles per convoy, and that will do the job."

"Roger," said the Air Force Commander and hung up the phone.

Shamir called the satellite control center. "Forget about the convoys," he told them. "Keep an eye only on the facility from which the convoys departed. I have a feeling the Iranians are trying to fool us with a double deception. First, they created a deception by splitting into three different convoys, and now they assume that if we destroy all three convoys, we will think we have destroyed the detonator, and therefore they did not even take it out of the facility.

"Watch the facility and update me if you detect any unusual activity."

Shamir hung up and called the Prime Minister on the encrypted line. He briefly updated him on the plan to destroy the three convoys and his bet that the detonator remained in the facility and was not destroyed.

"So how does this help us?" asked the Prime Minister.

"The Iranians will be certain we are convinced the detonator was destroyed and that we will stop looking for it. They will lower their alert level and be less cautious. I have a new plan to handle the problem. I need to consult with an expert, and if he approves my idea, I will present it to the Committee of Three tomorrow evening."

Danny cleared his throat. "I am back," he said. "I planted the beacons on all three convoys. I chose the middle truck in each convoy, just to be safe."

"Very good," said Shamir. "Go rest. Report here tomorrow at eight in the morning for the 'Lego' lesson and the meeting with the Committee of Three. Do not forget to bring the mask."

Danny left, and Shamir called Gershon Plank, chairman of the Nuclear Energy Committee.

"Call me urgently on a secure phone line," he requested.

After three minutes, the secure phone rang. "Gershon speaking. How can I help?"

"Two things," said Shamir. "First, tomorrow we will meet

with the Prime Minister in my command room at Mossad headquarters."

"And the second?" asked Gershon.

"I need to know how to sabotage the detonator without leaving signs," said Shamir.

"I will explain," said Gershon, "to cause atomic fission and thereby initiate a chain reaction that will ultimately lead to a nuclear explosion the bomb is built exactly like a soccer ball, one with patches in pentagonal shapes. The patches are made of regular explosive material, while the nuclear material meant to create the atomic explosion is located in the center of the ball.

Now, a technical explanation: to create the fission process of the nuclear material itself, let us say enriched uranium, for example. You simultaneously ignite the regular explosive material in the patches of our soccer ball.

"What is crucial in this explosion is that the explosion must be directed inward into the ball, thereby creating enormous symmetrical pressure on the uranium. The uranium core is compressed, and its density increases until creating pressure great enough to allow the process of fission of the uranium atom.

"If you want to sabotage this explosion, you have two options: First, reverse the explosion's direction so that the entire power of the regular explosive material is directed outward. The second option is to cause one of the patches not to explode, for instance by replacing it with an identical patch that is not made of explosive material.

"In such a case, the explosion would still be inward, but

because one patch is missing, it will not be symmetrical. The enormous pressure needed for the uranium atom to split will not reach the necessary intensity, and it will just be a regular bomb explosion, not an atomic explosion."

"Thank you," said Shamir. "You have helped me a lot. See you tomorrow evening at the 'Committee of Three' meeting."

Shamir hung up and called Avi, head of the Mossad's Technology Division.

"I need you to prepare a model of a nuclear detonator like the one the Iranians have by tomorrow morning," he told him.

"The model must be such that an agent can learn to disassemble the detonator and change the wiring or replace one of the ball's patches with another. Besides that, I need you to prepare one patch that looks exactly like the patch in the Iranians' detonator, and that no one would suspect is not the original patch."

"Understood, boss," said Avi. "We will start working immediately."

Shamir hung up the phone, took three deep breaths, and called the Air Force Commander.

"Did you receive the homing beacon transmission?"

"Yes, we received it, and we have already assigned a separate beacon to each pair of aircraft. According to the plan, in about half an hour, all that will remain of the three convoys will be nothing more than a heap of burnt metal and plastic."

"Good," said Shamir. "Update me after the attack is completed so I can report to the Prime Minister."

"Roger," said the Air Force Commander.

Throughout the day, Danny practiced disassembling and reassembling the nuclear detonator "Lego" like model, built during the night by the Mossad's Technology Division.

After dozens of times, he could open the ball, change the electrical wiring direction, and flip the direction outward.

Shamir explained to Danny that the first priority was to reverse the explosion direction from inward to outward by changing the wiring, but to be absolutely certain, Danny needed to be prepared to replace one of the patches with an innocent patch without explosive material.

At six in the evening that day, they sat in the command room at Mossad headquarters: the Prime Minister, the chairman of the Nuclear Energy Committee, the Head of the Mossad, and Danny, his face covered with a mask as usual.

The Head of the Mossad reviewed the situation. The three convoys were destroyed last night in a missile attack from Air Force planes. Satellite images received from the Americans near dawn show a smoking pile of scrap.

"We do not know if the detonator was in one of the convoys and destroyed in the attack, or if the Iranians tried to fool us and sent the convoys as a decoy, leaving the detonator in the 'Lavisan' facility."

Satellite photo analysis shows the fire of the attacked convoys was more or less uniform in size. If the nuclear detonator had been in one of the convoys, it would have exploded, and it is likely the fire remnants would have been larger in the convoy containing the detonator.

But this does not matter because our working assumption

since yesterday is that the nuclear detonator did not leave the facility and is still hidden there.

"How is it not important if the detonator is still intact and in Iranian hands?" asked Gershon, chairman of the Nuclear Energy Committee.

"We already understood yesterday that the detonator was probably not destroyed and remained in the facility. Therefore, I launched an action plan that will solve the nuclear detonator problem once and for all," said Shamir, Head of the Mossad.

What is the plan? asked the Prime Minister.

"We will not destroy the nuclear detonator," said the Head of the Mossad.

"Excellent plan," said the Prime Minister. "Do you have more plans like this? Maybe we will also replace the tank shells in the IDF with flowers?"

"We will not destroy it," said Shamir, "we will cause the Iranians to believe the nuclear detonator is healthy and intact, as Gershon mentioned, but in reality, we will sabotage it and prevent it from fulfilling its role."

"And how will we do that?" asked the Prime Minister.

Shamir described to the Prime Minister the detonator's structure, the internal explosion mechanism, the soccer ball-shaped patches, and the idea of either reversing the explosion direction or replacing one of the exploding patches with a patch without explosive material, thereby preventing the explosion from reaching the required intensity.

"If they activate the detonator, all that will happen is that it will explode in their face, along with the missile it is mounted on. All they will get out of it is a site contaminated with radioactive radiation that will spread in the facility and take them years to get rid of."

"Are you sure this will work?" asked the Prime Minister, looking at Gershon. "Is this soccer ball story real? Is this how it works?"

"Yes," Gershon answered, "this soccer ball is called the 'bomb core', and this is how it works."

"Excellent," said the Prime Minister. "Go."

CHAPTER SEVENTEEN:
EPILOGUE AND PERHAPS A BEGINNING

Two months later, Dina and Danny sat at twilight under an umbrella on comfortable chairs at 'Bograshov' Beach in Tel-Aviv.

On a small table between the chairs sat two "Mojito" cocktail glasses. "I am starting to get used to this drink," said Danny, sipping through the straw in the glass.

"Look at this interesting report that just popped up on my phone," said Dina, turning the cell phone screen towards him. On the screen appeared a headline: "Reuters News Agency reports that a mysterious explosion occurred last night at the nuclear site 'Lavisan' near Tehran. Iranian authorities stated it was an explosion of an old gas balloon, but satellite photos in our possession show extensive widespread destruction. Our science correspondent added that the UN Agency for Monitoring Nuclear Facilities in Iran reports that UN monitoring equipment installed at the facility as part of agreements to monitor nuclear weapons development showed an unusual spike in radioactive radiation levels at the facility."

Danny read the headline twice and smiled.

"What is funny?" asked Dina.

"Nothing, nothing," said Danny. "Just remembered a psalm verse we learned in 'yeshiva': 'He who digs a pit will fall into it.'"

"What does that mean?" Dina got irritated.

"It means that tonight, the people of Israel and the State of Israel can sleep much better," said Danny.

Danny's cell phone buzzed. "It is the boss," he told Dina. "I wonder what he wants from me now."

"Come here immediately," Shamir told him. "The President of the United States needs our help…"

End.

Printed in Great Britain
by Amazon